Sparx and Arrows

Dawn Vogel

CONTENTS

DADDY'S LITTLE GIRL

As Eleanor Castile reached the door to the study, she paused for a moment. She dropped her long skirt back into place and ran her hands over her hair, trying to mask the fact that she had been running. She calmed her breathing and reached for the door.

Off to the side, she heard someone clear his throat. She glanced over, ready to admonish her little brother, Edmond, that he should be in bed. The young man to the left of the door was not five-year-old Edmond, but rather someone about her own age. Recognition dawned as she realized that the man was the son of the new doctor. Eleanor tried to remember his name, but found herself at a loss. Something beginning with a B, she thought.

She exchanged quick pleasantries, consciously using formal address to skirt her lapse in memory. He followed her lead, and then they looked at each other awkwardly for a few long moments. Finally, Eleanor spoke again. "I must see my father."

Hiram Castile was surrounded by household servants and the doctor, who had been a regular visitor to the Castile household since his arrival in Cobalt City last winter. The servants moved aside as Eleanor approached, but the doctor remained by her father's side, tying a bandage on his left forearm. Eleanor pressed her eyes tightly shut at the sight of the crimson stain that already bloomed on the wrapping there.

Regardless of the cause, a forearm injury was a serious one for her father. While most of the world knew Hiram as simply an upstanding Cobalt City businessman and benefactor to the city, he frequently used the cover of darkness to take on the persona of his alter-ego, the Huntsman. Armed with a bow, he ensured that the streets of Cobalt City were safe for its citizens.

"Eleanor," he said in a thin, quiet voice, much different from his usual confident tone.

"Yes, Father, I'm here. What happened?"

Hiram glanced at the doctor. "Doctor Mathias, will you leave us for a moment?"

"Sir? Your wounds are ... substantial."

"I understand that, Doctor. I need to have a private word with my daughter. She is the lady of the house, after all. She needs to be informed of what is to be done."

Doctor Mathias stiffened, but nodded. "Very well, sir. I shall await her word before I return." He bowed formally, which Eleanor had barely enough presence of mind to acknowledge with a curtsy, and left the room.

Eleanor moved immediately to her father's side, and knelt beside the couch on which he lay. "Father, what happened?"

"Some sort of mechanical creations, fashioned to look like our former presidents. They're guarding a warehouse in Quayside, near the meat packing district. I couldn't get close enough to see much more than that. They're well-armed automatons, Eleanor. Far more resilient than others I've seen. Far too well armed to just be a normal security detail."

"What shall I do, then?"

"Victor is collecting a few samples of what their weapons did to our carriage, and you should take those, along with what I just told you, to your Uncle Louis."

"But Father, Uncle Louis has not had the full training! I have more training than he does!" Eleanor exclaimed.

"Yes, Eleanor. But if God sees fit to take me, and if Louis were to fail in this attempt, that makes you the only remaining Castile able to teach your brother what he needs to know to take up the mantle of the Huntsman."

Eleanor rose from her father's side and turned to stare out the window. "It's because I'm a girl, isn't it?"

Hiram did not answer immediately. Eleanor sighed inwardly, certain that her father would respond with some answer that made it seem that her safety was his primary concern. "Eleanor, you are my only daughter. I cannot send you out to finish what I was not able to do. Louis is prepared for such an eventuality." Hiram's voice broke with a sob. "I could never forgive myself if I lost you."

"If Edmond were 17, you would not hesitate to send him in your stead." She clapped her hand to her mouth as soon as she had spoken, shocked that she had voiced herself so forcefully.

Hiram sighed. "Perhaps you are right, Eleanor. However, that does not change my opinion. Louis will take care of this."

Eleanor composed her face carefully, and sat on the edge of the couch. She leaned forward and smoothed her father's hair. "As you wish, Father. You said the carriage was damaged in the attack?"

"Not severely damaged. Nothing that Victor won't have fixed by morning."

"I can ride to Uncle Louis's house before morning. I will take your equipment with me, and then he can begin work as soon as he arrives in Cobalt City. We'll have this taken care of before the doctor allows you to get out of bed."

"That's my girl," Hiram said, patting his daughter's arm gently. A grimace of pain slid across his face, and Eleanor rose.

"Doctor Mathias? My father needs you now." The door to the study opened immediately, as though the doctor had been waiting directly outside the entire time. Eleanor gave a quick curtsy and hurried into the hallway. The doctor's son was no longer waiting, but he had left a book in the chair he formerly occupied. She picked up the book idly, noting that it was one of the war treatises from her father's library. Her maid stood nearby, and Eleanor handed her the book. "Olivia, I need my riding habit ready in ten minutes and my horse in twenty. It appears I have a job to do."

~

Eleanor padded softly across the warehouse rooftop. In her left hand, she carried her father's bow. With her right hand, she clutched at the edges of her cloak, pulled tight to her body to help muffle the sound of the chain mail shirt she wore. The armor was too large for her, meant to fit her father's broad chest, but was surprisingly lightweight. Her eyes darted amongst the shadows on the rooftop, looking for any sign of movement other than her own. A strong wind rattled empty bottles and cans across the rough tarred surface, and wafted foul odors from the meat packing district and nearby warehouses. Eleanor remained still until the wind died down, trying to breathe through the edge of her hood to minimize the stench.

As she waited, she spotted a door on the rooftop. She moved slowly to the entrance and jiggled the doorknob. Finding it locked, she set to work with a hairpin as her father had taught her. The cylinders clicked into place, and Eleanor opened the door, which spilled a sliver of golden light across the rooftop. Eleanor froze, bowing her head slightly to keep her face obscured by the hood of the cloak, to ensure that her entrance was not noticed. After what seemed like more than a minute, she slipped through the doorway.

Inside the building, Eleanor moved more quickly. She tiptoed down a flight of well-lit stairs, seeking the shadows. She found them on a fragile looking catwalk of steel and wood, suspended high above the floor of the warehouse.

From her vantage point, the details of the work were not immediately apparent. She could see large bubbling vats that emanated an acrid stench, bathed in the glow of electrical lights. Two long work tables spanned the length of the warehouse. Each of these held metal parts, which workers were assembling into oversized rifles, far larger than a normal man could wield.

Around the perimeter of the work space, a group of automatons patrolled. As her father had told her, each of these was a mostly lifelike replica of one of the former Presidents of the United States. She could make out several versions of Abraham Lincoln, all wearing his signature stovepipe hat and keeping a close eye on the workers along the assembly line. Although Lincoln and the other former presidents looked to be life-sized, they carried the bulky rifles with ease.

Eleanor leaned slightly over the railing of the catwalk, trying to get a better look at the end of Ulysses S. Grant's cigar, which glowed orange, but emitted no smoke. One of the James Madison automatons swiveled his head completely around, and pointed in her direction. George Washington and Thomas Jefferson took aim with their rifles, and Eleanor tried to duck.

Before she could move, however, a strong arm grabbed her from behind. She felt her feet lift off of the catwalk just as a hail of bullets tore through the wooden beams. A moment later, Eleanor landed on another part of the catwalk, protected from the gunfire by a thick brick wall. The arm around her waist released her as

4

soon as she had her footing.

Eleanor spun around to face her assailant. The man standing behind her was dressed much like she was. He wore a long cloak with the hood pulled up, but obscured the top half of his face with a small domino mask in solid black. He held a single finger to his lips in warning, and then glanced at the bow.

"Huntsman?" he asked. "I didn't think you'd be up and about so quickly."

"I'm a quick healer. Why did you move me?" she whispered, trying to keep her voice both quiet and deeper than normal.

"You looked like you were about to get shot," the man suggested with a shrug. "You're lighter than I expected."

"I'm glad I am," Eleanor huffed. "You might have dropped me otherwise."

The man's eyes widened slightly, but he said nothing in response.

"This is hardly fair. You know who I am, and knew that I'd been injured, but I haven't a clue who you are. How do I know you're not working for whoever runs this place?"

"I, er... I'm a bit new to this scene." The faintest hint of a blush crept across his lower face. "In fact, this is the first time I've tried this whole defender of the people thing."

Eleanor tried to hide her smile. "What shall I call you?"

"How about Booth?" He suggested, a smile spreading across his face. "I was thinking it might be about time to pay our ex-presidents a quick visit from above. I wonder if I'd be hailed as a murderer or a savior in this case?"

"I wouldn't recommend it, either way. It'd be a nasty fall."

"Falling is for amateurs. I descend and ascend with perfect grace."

Eleanor walked away without replying, rolling her eyes as she went. She stepped to the edge of the brickwork, trying to see what had transpired below. Several of the automatons had clustered beneath the spot where they had shot out the catwalk, but they had not yet located the hiding pair. Production continued unabated, though another human had joined the workers. This one carried a sheaf of blueprints in one hand, while his other hand adjusted a monocle covering his right eye.

"That's Gregor Timonov," Eleanor muttered. "So that answers the question of who made the automatons."

"But why with the faces of ex-Presidents? And what's so interesting about those guns?"

"I haven't worked that part out yet. What do you do other than graceful falling?"

Booth reached for one edge of his cloak and drew it back, revealing row upon row of tiny snug pockets, each containing a shining vial filled with a liquid or powder. "Chemical compounds. I've got a little bit of everything here. What are you looking for?"

Eleanor smiled, reaching for one of her arrows. "How about a quick distraction while I snatch those plans?"

Booth selected two vials from his cloak and edged along the catwalk to a clear vantage point. Eleanor nocked an arrow attached to an almost imperceptibly thin length of cord. "Say the word," Booth whispered.

"On three," Eleanor replied, and then tapped her foot in three steady beats. She loosed the arrow as Booth hurled both of his vials toward the factory floor.

Their timing proved impeccable. Her arrow pierced the center of the plans just as a large cloud of white smoke blossomed up from Timonov's feet. As he and the other workers began coughing, Eleanor gave the cord a quick tug, and her arrow and the plans flew out of the smoke and directly into her hand.

She turned to Booth with a smile. "Now, to find someone to read these."

~

Eleanor glanced around before she climbed down from her horse. The alleys of Cobalt City were dark, and she was certain that she had not been followed, but she knew that it was best to remain on the alert at all times.

Booth had remained at the warehouse, trying to learn more about the automatons, while Eleanor had taken the blueprints to an old family friend. She had implored Booth to not do anything rash in her absence, but the acrobatic chemist's eyes had gleamed when he promised to behave. She hoped she would not find him dead or the warehouse no longer standing.

As she rounded the corner, she exhaled gently. The warehouse was intact. But the rope that Booth had dropped out a window for her speedy exit was no longer hanging down the side of the building. Eleanor's eyes darted to the window where the rope should have been, and saw it neatly coiled on the ledge. She began to curse Booth under her breath, when a hint of movement at ground level caught her eye.

Two of the automatons, replicas of Andrew Jackson and Zachary Taylor, rounded the corner of the building. Their measured steps and swiveling heads reminded Eleanor of tin soldiers on parade. Both of the automatons rested large rifles against one shoulder, like sentries.

Rather than continuing around the perimeter of the building, however, the automatons stopped near the spot where she had landed. Jackson bent at the waist and studied the ground, while Taylor's head continued to rotate.

"Time to see what these things are really made of," she muttered as she aimed an arrow at Taylor's right eye. It hit solidly, creating a spray of sparks and stopping the construct dead in its tracks. Jackson did not look up, even when Taylor began emitting a high pitched whine. A thin stream of steam erupted from the hole created by her arrow.

At the exact instant that Taylor's head exploded, Jackson moved. He flowed effortlessly to Taylor's side and seized the now non-functional automaton's weapon. Stabilizing himself on one knee, he hefted a rifle in each hand, and Eleanor found herself staring at the business ends of two of the oversized rifles.

She froze for only half a second, then dropped into a low crouch. The muzzles of the weapons followed her movement. "Old Hickory" pulled the triggers, but his weapons did not fire.

Taking advantage of the guns' malfunction, Eleanor sighted an arrow and aimed for Jackson's right eye. Without pausing to draw breath, she loosed the arrow. Jackson's fingers twitched on both triggers, but Eleanor had rolled out of the way before bullets began clattering out of the barrels.

"Ladies first, then," Eleanor murmured.

She waited long enough to see the second automaton's head combust, and then moved forward to examine the weapons. She did not attempt to lift either, but simply looked them over for the several joins that her father's friend had pointed out. At the base of each barrel, a narrow gap allowed the volatile bullets to "breathe." Satisfied, she closed the distance to the wall, where she found Booth watching out the window. He lowered the rope and Eleanor began to climb, soon aided by Booth pulling the rope hand over hand.

She climbed through the window unaided. "The weapons are modified Gatling guns. They probably weigh fifty or sixty pounds each, so that explains why the automatons are wielding them. The ammunition has magnesium in its core..."

"So it makes a bright light when it hits the air. Not quite sure about the practical application of that," Booth mused. Suddenly, he snapped his fingers. "Oh, but it will burn like the devil himself, especially if we can get it wet!"

"That's what my source believes as well. So Timonov has created his own personal army, more powerful than anyone else in the city. Luckily, the guns can be destroyed with an accurate shot, but I'm not sure about the automatons. Either way, once I hit one of either, it's likely to bring unwanted attention."

Booth rummaged through the tiny pockets lining his cloak. "Can you fire an accurate shot if there's a small vial attached to your arrow?"

"I believe so. What will the vial do?"

"Ignite the bullets, make the rifle explode. If we're lucky, trigger a few of the nearby rifles to do the same. Maybe take off a few of the automaton's heads in the process. That does seem to shut them down."

"Then you need to make sure that the workers have left the building before I start firing. Give me the vials and ten minutes to get them attached."

"Make it twenty if you want everyone human out. They change shifts at midnight. I should be able to have a few constables here by then. And you'll want to be ready to get out yourself, preferably unseen and unharmed." Booth's hand lingered on Eleanor's as he handed her the fragile vials. She tried to put his charming smile out of her mind as she began assembling her arrows.

~

Eleanor slid her finger across one of the modified arrows, testing its balance. Finally satisfied, she waited for the chiming of the St. Alban's bells. As soon as they began to toll the midnight hour, Eleanor readied her bow. Booth had been correct about the workers, as they all filed toward the entrance of the warehouse. She sighted along the arrow to locate the vulnerable point on one of the guns, and fired. Booth's vial shattered on impact, and the gun exploded in a burst of white light that quickly transformed into fierce flames. Eleanor found herself smiling at how effective the arrow had been as three more guns suffered a similar fate, all from the flames of the first.

She reached for another arrow, but found that she could not draw the one she grasped from the quiver. She reached for another, but it was similarly stuck in place. In frustration, she tugged harder, mangling the feathers at the end. The arrow finally pulled free, but as she moved to nock the arrow, she realized that the vial she had so carefully tied to the arrow was missing. She slipped the quiver from her back and began looking at her arrows. The vial had been crushed by the pressure of her pulling the arrow out, and the contents were rapidly saturating the nearby arrows with whatever chemical Booth had provided her. With a faint cry, she dumped the contents of the quiver onto the catwalk, and began salvaging the arrows that were still intact.

Below her on the warehouse floor, the automatons moved around and scanned the upper portions of the space. With only five arrows pulled from the wreckage of the quiver, the sounds of gunfire forced Eleanor to roll away from her position. The gunfire continued, filling the air with an almost sulfurous odor.

Eleanor yelped as her legs plunged into empty space. She reminded herself again that she needed to locate men's pants that would fit, as her skirt caught on a splintered board, arresting her downward motion. She found herself flailing about as she tried to get a grasp on the nearby catwalk before additional bullets came her way.

Eleanor looked around, panic evident on her face. Booth slipped in through one of the upper windows and surveyed the situation. A flash of fear slipped across his normally jocular features, but he quickly mastered it. He tossed a hook and rope at one of the ceiling crossbeams, then swung across the open space to lift Eleanor out of her predicament.

As he set her down on solid catwalk for the second time tonight, he murmured into her ear. "Huntsman, I realize you're a well-respected hero, but perhaps you should leave the lacy drawers at home when you're investigating crimes."

Eleanor gasped and looked down at her dress, which had fallen back into place over her underclothing. Her face felt hot as she arranged the cloak to cover the sizable rip in her riding clothing. She kept her face hidden, too embarrassed even to speak. Booth similarly remained silent.

After a long minute, Eleanor looked up to try to explain herself to Booth. Beyond his shoulder, she saw Timonov, flanked by two of his automatons. "Hide," she whispered. Booth ducked into the shadows, trying to pull her along with him.

Eleanor remained standing on the catwalk, the ruined portion between her and Timonov. She held her father's bow loosely in her left hand, and the remaining arrows in her right. As Timonov drew closer, he saw both. "Huntsman. I should have known that it was you who disrupted my patrolmen earlier. And now you've come back to seal your fate?"

Just off to her left, Booth whispered. "Keep your face covered. I'll do the talking." Then, a voice just as deep as Timonov's answered. "Timonov. Run now, while you have the chance." Eleanor darted a quick glance in Booth's direction and saw that he had found a long tube, through which he was speaking. The tube amplified and deepened his voice to a good approximation of Hiram Castile at his best.

"Why should I run when I have you cornered, Huntsman?"

Before Booth could speak again, Eleanor had raised the bow and all five arrows. "Because I'm faster than those hunks of metal," she snapped, the tautness of her voice echoing the twang of the bow string.

Timonov's scream and two hissing sounds informed her of the accuracy of her shots. Looking up, she saw that the central arrow had pierced Timonov's monocle, while the two arrows to either side had scored direct hits on the heads of the automatons. As steam leaked from the automaton's heads, blood began flowing from Timonov's eye.

Booth turned to look out the window, and used his makeshift speaking horn to call out to the constables below. With no arrows remaining, Eleanor faded back into the shadows with Booth and let the constabulary finish the job.

~

Eleanor slipped into the house through the servant's entrance, and was surprised to see her father sitting on a divan in the hallway. "Father, shouldn't you be in bed?"

"Shouldn't you still be on your way to Louis's estate?"

Eleanor hung her head. "I'm sorry. I went to the warehouse against your wishes. I just ..."

"Constable Cooper stopped by on his way home to drop off the Huntsman's quiver, since I know our beloved hero. He said Huntsman did a 'bang up' job of catching Timonov." Hiram paused. "Thank you."

"What?" Eleanor looked up, stunned.

"Thank you for ensuring that the people of Cobalt City know that they can count on the Huntsman. I didn't want you to risk your life in my stead, but it seems that perhaps my fears were unfounded. You have the skills necessary to be the Huntsman, and you bore the mantle well."

Eleanor choked back a sob as she rushed to hug her father.

"Doctor Mathias says that I should rest for at least three weeks before I take up my nocturnal activities again. If you promise me that you will call for help whenever you need it, you may take on the role until I have healed."

"Oh, I promise! Thank you, Father! Thank you! I've even found someone who I can call on for help, and you will be able to call on him as well."

Hiram kissed Eleanor's cheek through the tears of joy that streamed down her face. "Wonderful, you can tell me all about him later. Now, help me into that ridiculous wheelchair that the doctor left. It's not as though my legs are badly hurt. But he'll be very cross with me if his son reports back to him that I've been walking around."

"His son?"

"Yes. I'm not certain why, but he sent his son, Booth, over just a few minutes ago."

Eleanor gasped. "Doctor Mathias's son's name is Booth?"

"Yes," Hiram replied slowly. "Curious, Olivia said that he asked after you first, but I told her that I would see him. It's not proper for a young man to call on a young lady at this time of night, regardless of the errand. Do you know him?"

"I don't, but the Huntsman does," Eleanor answered with a twinkle in her eye.

"Daddy's Little Girl" first appeared in *Cobalt City Timeslip*.

RED SCARE

Sarah Castile glared at the telegram. She'd agreed to take on a special assignment in Italy for a number of reasons, the foremost being the pleasant autumn weather. The rest of Europe was ghastly this time of year. And now, the remnant Allied network she'd thrown her lot in with wanted her to pack up and go to Russian-occupied Germany, of all places. Neither her German nor her Russian accents were up to snuff. She'd have to spend the journey practicing.

Once before, a many-times-great aunt had become the Huntsman in a time of need. If a worldwide war did not qualify as a time of need, Sarah had no idea what did. Her brother had inherited the mantle of the Huntsman as the men in her family had done for over a century and a half. But while he remained in Cobalt City protecting the home front, she had packed her own bow and quiver beneath layers of blankets in the supply bins for the voyage across the Atlantic. She had tried to keep her activities as clandestine as possible, but of course the war correspondents telegraphed home about the Huntsman's deeds in Europe. Speculation abounded as to how he could be two places at once, though more than a few correctly suspected there was more than one Huntsman.

With quick motions, Sarah folded the telegram as small as she could and tucked it into her handbag. The small "mg" in the bottom corner elicited a momentary smile. At least Mary had retained a position at Bletchley Park. It was nice to get less than pleasant assignments from someone so cordial.

She squinted against the bright October sun as she composed three telegrams in her head. It was simple enough to write to her father and let him know that her sojourn would be extended. In many ways, she suspected such correspondence gave him great relief, not needing to worry about his errant daughter and her tradition-bucking ways. Similarly, her telegram to the command center at Bletchley Park would not require much work either--a simple "agreed" would prompt them to go forward with the next phase of their plan.

It was the third telegram that caused her the most turmoil, though she tried to convince herself that it was camaraderie, not affection, that made her feel that way. The Huntsman's activities in Europe had caught not only the attention of the press, but also that of a different sort of hero who had made Italy his base of operations for centuries, though without passing the helm from generation to generation. The Venetian was a vampire, who had enlisted the Huntsman's help to take out a particularly nasty nest of his kinsmen near Paris before the war ended. Since then, the Huntsman and the Venetian had traveled the Continent, fighting vampires and worse monsters. And it was the telegram to the Venetian that caused Sarah the most hesitation.

In the end, she went with a simple, unapologetic message: "Needed elsewhere. Will return soon. -H-"

~

Sarah stepped out onto the platform at the train station in Leipzig, her gaze sweeping across the crowd for her contact. The Freedom Alliance Network had no designated signals to connect their agents, but each individual agent had a signature item, easily identified even among the newest agents. Sarah pulled her vivid green scarf up to cover her hair and protect from the chilly wind. As she did, she saw a woman on the other side of the station don a wide-brimmed plum hat, which stood out starkly against the black and drab colors that most of the passengers wore. Sarah picked up her small travelling satchel and slung the guitar case that carried her bow and quiver across her back in one fluid motion.

The flow of the crowd was such that Sarah could not make her way to the other agent without causing a stir, so she followed along with the other departing passengers. An elderly couple in front of her moved particularly slowly, and she took a moment to look at the buildings near the train station. A flash of bright red fabric fluttering in the wind drew her gaze back to one of the taller buildings, but whatever had been flapping around was already gone. Sarah could not recall any agents in the Network who wore red--the connections between the color and Russian Communism seemed close enough to make it taboo.

Across the platform, the woman in the plum hat appeared to identify Sarah's inability to reach her and began moving toward the street. It was not until they reached the sidewalk in front of the station that they were able to meet.

"Magda, so good to see you!" Sarah's preferred dialect was Austrian German, which meant that what little accent she could manage sounded good enough for a crowded city street.

The other woman leaned in to kiss Sarah on both cheeks, and murmured, "It's Illyana, actually. You are Sarah?"

"Lizbet if you need a name to say aloud," Sarah replied, her voice low.

As the two women separated from their embrace, Illyana smiled at Sarah. "I trust your journey was good?"

"Yes, but I would like to get out of this weather." Sarah peered up at the gray sky. "Winter will be here too soon."

"It always is," Illyana said, tucking her arm through Sarah's. "Come, I am staying not far from here."

The two women walked and chatted amiably, just as two old friends might. As they did, Sarah tried to recall anything she knew about Illyana. The name was most certainly Russian, which worried Sarah, but she reminded herself that not all Russians agreed with their leaders. At any rate, unless Illyana was leading her into a trap with overwhelming odds, Sarah was confident in her ability to best the Russian woman.

Of more concern was the prickling of the hairs on the back of her neck. She had not seen any more glimpses of red on the rooftops, but she could not be sure that any tail they had was still above street level. Sarah paused in front of one of the shops that she and Illyana were passing, admiring a display of hearty bread beneath a sign advertising cakes. "The war has been hard on Leipzig," Illyana said with a sigh.

15

"It has been hard everywhere," Sarah said. Her gaze flickered across the nearby windows, but no one stood out as an obvious threat. She leaned closer to Illyana. "I feel as though I'm being watched."

"You probably are," Illyana murmured. "Austria is ... far from here, on many levels."

"I assure you, if I were speaking Russian, I would sound far worse."

"Then let me do the talking." Illyana steered Sarah away from the window and down a side street, launching into an expert elaboration on the architecture of the buildings that lined the narrow cobble street.

The feeling of being watched persisted, but Sarah was not in a position that allowed her to get a good glimpse of whether or not they were being followed. So she nodded as Illyana talked, and limited her speech to only the simplest of German words while they remained on the street.

Sarah let out a small sigh of relief when they arrived at Illyana's building. Inside was a cozy yet Spartan apartment.

Illyana cruised around the space, adjusting the curtains carefully. "Your scarf must be soaked," she said, helping Sarah out of it. She then carefully draped it across the curtain rod of the front window, effectively blocking anyone's line of sight into the sitting room of the apartment. "Better?"

"Much, thank you." Sarah perched on the edge of a solid wooden chair. "Now then, I expect we have much more to discuss."

"Indeed," Illyana replied, dropping into thickly accented English. "Recent intercepted communications from Mother Russia say that German scientists are to be moved into Russian cities. Many do not wish to go, but it will not be possible to prevent all of them from being taken. But the Network has a list of those that must be retrieved at any cost."

Sarah frowned. "And they needed me for this?"

Illyana shrugged. "You liberated Malthausen-Gusen during the war, yes?"

"Yes, but not on my own. I had backup." *And tanks.*

"You have backup here too."

Sarah looked at Illyana closely. Based on their walking speed, Sarah judged the Russian woman to be more physically fit than her baggy clothing let on. But Sarah had seen no evidence that Illyana was anything more than healthy and well fed for this part of the world. "What is it that you do?"

"Many things. But for the purposes of this mission? I am on the inside. This Russian operation is much like your American Project Paperclip. And as far as they know, I am a part of their bureaucratic machine." Illyana rose and went into the kitchen. When Sarah did not follow immediately, she poked her head out. "There is no table in the sitting room large enough to finish my explanation."

Sarah followed Illyana into a room that barely looked useable for the preparation of meals. Every surface--both horizontal and vertical--was covered with maps, blueprints, and other plans. Snippets of at least a dozen different languages peppered the various pieces of paper.

The Russian woman picked up a long stick and began pointing as she spoke. "Our quarry is a physicist by the name of Doctor Berthold Funken. He is to be loaded onto a train here in Leipzig on the twenty-second of October. I will be on that train, and will locate Doctor Funken. You will await the train's arrival about ten kilometers east of Dresden. You will watch for a purple flag hanging out the window of one of the cars, and then will decouple the train cars behind that car. I will escort Doctor Funken and his wife from the train, and you and I will take them back to Dresden, where a boat will get them up the Elbe and then out of Germany. Understood?"

Sarah frowned as she followed Illyana's pointer across the map. "If we need to get him to Dresden to catch a boat, why not just get him off the train in Dresden?"

Illyana shook her head. "Too many Russian soldiers in Dresden, occupied with rebuilding. The boat will be far enough outside of the city that it will be safe. And, of course, you will be there to help guard Doctor Funken."

"Alright, that seems reasonable. What do the trains use for their coupling mechanism?"

"Are you familiar with the SA-3?"

"That's the interlocking one, right?"

Illyana nodded.

"Nothing a little light explosive can't take care of, then."

~

Sarah hurried from Illyana's apartment toward the hotel that the other agent had directed her to. The drizzly gray weather had driven her to pull her scarf over her hair again. With no peripheral vision, she nearly collided with another pedestrian.

"Oh, I beg your pardon," she exclaimed in German, pulling the edge of her scarf aside to look at the other person.

The face beneath the wide brimmed hat that smiled back at her was one she had not expected to see.

"*Tesoro,*" the Venetian said, embracing Sarah.

She returned the vampire's embrace stiffly, muttering "What are you doing here?" in his native Italian as she did.

He shrugged as he took her arm and responded in kind. "I could not have you wandering around this part of Germany unescorted."

Sarah wanted to extricate herself from the Venetian's arm, but his grip was like an iron manacle. "How did you even know that I was here?"

"I ... that is ... well ..." he stammered. When he composed his thoughts, his voice was significantly softer. "I followed the scent of your perfume. I didn't mean to annoy you, I just thought that such an abrupt message might mean that you had gotten into some sort of trouble that you couldn't convey via telegram."

Sarah sighed. "Your intentions are noble, V, but I'm perfectly fine. I've got work to do here. And believe it or not, I'm actually capable of taking care of myself."

"Yes, of course you are," he replied. "It was foolish of me to think otherwise."

"Shouldn't you be sleeping this time of day, anyway?"

He gestured to the wide-brimmed hat. "Between this and the weather, I don't feel the need."

"I'm surprised you haven't moved to Norway, what with your dislike of the sun."

"Ah, but could I convince you to join me there? I think not, unless there were trolls to hunt. Italy is home, and you like it there. So I stay."

Sarah's brow creased with a combination of frustration and confusion. She was never certain if the Venetian was just an unrepentant flirt, or if he actually cared about her. Either way, having him here while she was on Network business was an unneeded complication. "Well, I should be done with my work in a few days. But in the meantime ..." She indicated the hotel with a tilt of her head. "I should get to it."

"May I offer my assistance?"

She smiled stiffly. "I'll be heading to Dresden tomorrow. Would you be so kind as to get me a ticket?"

The Venetian frowned, but nodded. "Of course, *Tesoro*."

Her smile remained tight as she wriggled out from the vampire's grip. "Thank you, good evening."

Once inside the hotel, Sarah released a long, slow sigh. She muddled her way through the transaction with the desk clerk, barely able to keep her mind thinking in German. Her thoughts returned to the Venetian. She had no good way to ask him to go home without upsetting him. And she could not bring herself to do that.

~

Dresden had but one functioning hotel, and Sarah located it on her arrival the next day. One of the wings was still being reconstructed, and the proprietor of the hotel was confused when she requested a room as near to that area as possible. "Oh, the noise won't bother me." She patted her guitar case. "Anyway, I'm a musician, and I don't want to bother your other guests."

The proprietor smiled stiffly and led her to the requested room.

After settling into her room, she took to the rubble-strewn streets in search of a telegraph office. The workmen watched her as she went, and she wished she had changed into something less noticeable. Then again, her old uniform would have probably attracted just as much attention, but of a different tenor.

The telegram she wrote was brief. "M. Direct correspondence to room 204, Altstadt, Dresden. Here 2 days more."

She made her way back to her hotel, feeling as though she was being watched even more than she had on the streets of Leipzig. She tried to catch a glimpse of her pursuer, checking both the street and what few rooftops remained, but saw no one particularly suspicious. Still, the sense of eyes on her abated only when she ascended to the second floor in the hotel.

Her heart skipped a beat when she saw the door to her room

hung ajar. While her service pistol was in her handbag, she preferred her bow. With no other choice at the moment, she drew her gun and circumvented the worst of the crumbling plaster chunks strewn across the hallway.

Pausing just outside her room, she nudged the door farther open with the toe of her shoe. She'd put her guitar case in the large standing wardrobe, which she could see from the doorway. Its door remained closed, and her bag was still where she had left it on the bed. A gust of wind brought with it a fine dust of plaster, and Sarah shielded her eyes with her left arm, still holding her gun steady with the right. Something or someone brushed past her, but by the time she moved her arm away from her eyes, whatever or whoever it had been was gone.

Sarah strode into her room and closed the window, which had been locked when she departed. Perhaps it had been a maid wanting to air the room out a bit after her unexpected arrival. But she was on edge now. She poked her head back out into the hallway but found no one there.

Closing the door firmly behind her and engaging the lock, she proceeded to check every nook and cranny in her room for any signs of an intruder. Despite the fine layer of plaster dust covering the entire room, there were no foot or finger prints. A cold chill washed down Sarah's spine. The Venetian was capable of entering a room and leaving no trace, but there was no reason for him to be skulking around her room in Dresden. But other vampires were a strong possibility.

Sarah tidied up the plaster dust as best as she could, sweeping it out into the hallway with a sheaf of hotel stationery. Then she wedged the desk chair under the doorknob, and rummaged through her bag for anything that she might put on the windowsill in the hopes that it would fall and wake her if the window was opened while she slept. Finding nothing, she opened her guitar case and removed the arrowheads from several of her arrows, setting the metal and rubber pieces in a row on the window sill.

With her quiver of remaining arrows and her bow, she propped herself up in the bed, piling pillows behind her. Sleeping sitting up was not the most restful way to pass a night, but it would do.

After a fitful night of sleep, Sarah returned to the front desk. Sunlight streamed through the front doors, catching on millions of dust motes swirling through the air. She placed a small stack of *lire* on the countertop and smiled at the desk clerk. "I need to leave unexpectedly. This should cover my room for another night, and there's a bit extra there. If any telegrams come addressed to my room, could you please send a response that I left a day ahead of schedule?"

~

Sarah saw the steam from the train's engine long before the train was in view. She had found a good vantage point on a hill that the tracks had been built around rather than through, a ruined structure atop it, and she had her exploding tip arrows ready to fire.

As the train drew nearer, she could tell that something was wrong. The engine pulled only a few cars, and all of them were filled to the brim with coal. She was certain she had followed the correct tracks out of Dresden, but now she wondered if a change in plans might have been communicated to the hotel after she had departed. And while Illyana was somehow involved in the project to move the German scientists to Russia, Sarah doubted that the Russian woman was highly placed enough to alter train schedules.

A rustling behind her drew her attention, and Sarah whirled to find herself face to face with the Venetian.

"V, what are you doing here? Did you follow me again?"

"I did, but this time I have a message related to the matter at hand. The train carrying your quarry was rerouted north, to Berlin."

"Did Illyana tell you this?"

"No, it was in a telegram delivered to your room. At the hotel."

Sarah frowned. Her mind was awhirl with questions, but she wasn't certain where to begin. If the telegram the Venetian had seen was accurate, then there was no way she could stop the train carrying Doctor Funken before it reached Berlin. There was far too much territory to cover, and the train had a headstart. But it seemed unlikely to her that Illyana would transmit information of that sort in a telegram. "Do you have the telegram with you?" she asked.

"Of course." The Venetian handed her a neatly folded telegram with her former hotel and room number printed on the outside.

Sarah looked over the contents of the telegram, and immediately saw what the men at the hotel would not have. Though the telegram itself was in German, the words that would

21

begin with lowercase letters if handwritten spelled out "Delayed" in English. She grinned at the Venetian. "You missed the ..."

Before she could finish, the Venetian swept in and pulled her close to him. Near enough to kiss her, he whispered in rapid-fire Italian. "I was followed. I understand the message. We must wait elsewhere."

As if to punctuate his quick message, the sound of falling rocks caught Sarah's attention. "Too late," she said, crouching to scoop up her explosive arrows and put them back in her quiver. She grabbed instead a smoke screen arrow and fired it at the ground in the direction of the falling rocks. The resultant cloud of smoke obscured the approaching soldiers, but it also hid Sarah and the Venetian from the view of their potential attackers.

Sarah looked up at the Venetian and smiled. "Shall we make our exit?"

He glanced behind them, down the opposite side of the hill. "I'm afraid we missed our chance. I believe my pursuers were Russian. What level of response do you think is appropriate?"

Sarah sighed and located one of her rubber-tipped arrows. "No reason to kill them, I'm afraid."

"I doubt they will show us the same courtesy," the Venetian replied. "But I will follow your lead in this."

As soon as Sarah saw one of the Russian uniform caps crest the hill, she loosed her arrow. She plugged the first Russian in the temple, and he crumpled. The rubber-tipped arrows might be non-lethal, but they packed a strong enough punch to knock a man out.

The first hail of bullets from the Russians, fired wildly at the top of the hill, drove Sarah into a crouching position. The Venetian flitted around her, whirling his long cape into the path of the bullets and slowing them down.

"I'm not going to get a clean shot if you keep getting in my way," Sarah grumbled.

"You also won't get a clean shot if you are hit, *Tesoro.*"

"I'll be fine." She rolled and came up behind one of the remaining partial walls atop the hill. "See? Fine."

"Good. Now watch your back, as I believe they have us surrounded." The Venetian leapt away, defying gravity as he floated lazily back to the hilltop.

Sarah alternated between creating smoke screens and knocking out the Russian soldiers who made it past the concealment. She had to choose her targets carefully, as she hadn't brought an extensive supply of either type of arrow with her. But between her arrows and the Venetian's fists and kicks, they were keeping the Russians from gaining the high ground.

The stones of the wall that provided cover ground against each other alarmingly. Sarah rolled to safety as the top few stones crumbled and fell into the spot where she had just been. A wave of force punched into her back. A moment later, the world around her exploded. She could not hear, and all she saw was a bright white light. "Oh, don't tell me all of the preachers were right about what happens when you die," she muttered. But she felt the rumbling in her throat from her words, and she suspected that was a sign she was still alive.

A moment later her vision cleared. The Venetian stood over her, his eyes wide, shaking her shoulder.

"What?" Sarah shouted, unable to hear even herself.

The Venetian's lips moved slowly, and his words were in English. "The train! Now!"

Sarah rolled to her feet, ignoring the pounding of her head and the spots of light still dancing in her vision. She saw the train she had expected earlier, and there was the purple flag waving in the wind. "Keep them off me," she shouted, vehemently enough that her throat burned. She hoped the Venetian could still hear. And she hoped that the Russians didn't get any crazy ideas about using more grenades.

Sarah had to steady herself against the crumbling wall, now even more precariously situated. She sighted along the top of her exploding arrow, training it on the flag at first. As the train approached, she lowered her bow slightly so that she now watched at the level where the coupling would appear. She would have only a single chance to hit her target, and with the way the train danced before her eyes, she wasn't too pleased with the odds.

She paused as she realized a different plan than the one she had discussed with Illyana. She had only one shot if she aimed for the coupling behind the car with the flag. But there was no reason she knew of that she could not decouple the train in front of that car instead. And if she missed that shot, she'd get another chance to stop the car that Doctor Funken was in.

The coupling that attached the car with Illyana's flag to the rest of the train slid into view, and Sarah fired. As soon as the arrow was loosed, she already had another explosive arrow nocked.

The first arrow hit the door of the car in front of the one Illyana had marked. Sarah took a deep breath and let it out as the first arrow exploded. The cars did not decouple.

She aimed again, adjusting her shot based on how the first had flown. When she loosed the second arrow, she smiled. This one would fly true.

The explosion from the second arrow finally pierced the silence with a muffled boom. But the car behind the one waving Illyana's purple flag, and all those behind it, began to slow while the rest of the train steamed on.

~

Sarah kept watch from the deck of the ship as it steamed up the Danube. Behind her, someone approached with a deliberately heavy tread. She glanced over her shoulder and smiled at the Venetian. "I thought you were supposed to be a master of stealth."

"I am," he replied. "I didn't want you to think I was trying to sneak up on you again. Nor did I want you to think the Russians had 'gotten the drop' on us."

The Venetian's use of the American colloquialism sounded ridiculous, and Sarah laughed in spite of herself. "Sorry. I assume you came up here for a reason."

He nodded. "He wants to meet you."

The Venetian didn't have to indicate who "he" was. Sarah knew it was Doctor Funken. "Of course. Lead the way."

Sarah followed the Venetian to one of the small cabins below deck. Inside, Illyana sat with a remarkably young looking couple. Had the woman not been visibly pregnant, Sarah would have had a hard time believing they were even teenagers.

The young man beamed at her. "Our savior," he said in thickly accented English.

"It's a pleasure, Doctor Funken. I'm glad we were able to help."

"You did much more than help. You've ensured that our family will have a bright future in the land of the free." He paused. "They tell me you liberated Malthausen-Gusen?"

Sarah glanced at the Venetian, who hid his sly smile with his coat collar. "I was a part of the liberation. Were you there?"

Doctor Funken shook his head. "No, but I had dear friends

who were. They live because of you. You are truly a hero."

Sarah blushed, awkward under the attention of everyone in the room. "Glad I could help. But enough about me. What are your plans when you reach America?"

Doctor Funken's wife spoke up, her English less accented than that of her husband. "The first order of business is to find a good doctor to deliver our child."

"If you don't mind a bit of overland travel when you get to New York, I can recommend a good physician in Cobalt City. He comes from a long line of doctors."

"Cobalt City, eh?" Doctor Funken asked. "I don't suppose they have any private sector jobs for rocket scientists? I am through with working for the military."

"I might know a few people who could be persuaded to hire you. I'll write you some letters of introduction." Sarah smiled. "And if nothing else, there are also a number of heroes in Cobalt City who would be happy to make use of your services in the name of justice. If you're interested, of course."

UNEXPECTED SPARX

Kara Sparx groaned as she rolled out of bed. Sleeping on her guest bedroom mattress for a few days had made her realize just how horrible it was. With her sister and niece in town, Kara had decided the two of them should share the master suite, while she slept in the tiny downstairs bedroom ostensibly reserved for guests. Of course, Kara was the first person to sleep on the guest bed. Most of her old friends had a wide array of choices as to where they would stay when they visited Cobalt City. When family came, though, it only made sense to let them stay with her.

As Kara stretched and winced at the popping noises of her back, she noticed that the house seemed oddly quiet. She glanced at the clock and realized that she had slept nearly until noon. After waking up by eight the past two mornings, she guessed she needed the extra sleep. But she had been awoken on those mornings by her niece, Bridget. On the first morning, the seven-year-old girl had been digging through Kara's toolbox. The second morning, she had tried to hook up one of Kara's amplifiers. Bridget's mother, Denise, had managed to stop her daughter on both occasions, but the noise didn't let Kara sleep as late as she was accustomed to.

Kara reached for her cell phone and checked for messages. Finding none, she called Denise's cell phone, half listening to see if she could hear her sister's ridiculous pop song ringtone in the house.

"Hello?" Denise's voice was distorted by a heavy wind.

"Denise? Did you and Bridget go out?"

"Oh, yeah. We didn't want to wake you. Bridget kept seeing those carnival posters everywhere, and she promised to be extra quiet this morning if I took her."

Kara groaned inwardly. "Denise, I told you the carnival was a bad idea."

"I know, but you've seen how Bridget can get. I didn't want her to get into your stuff again. I figured we'd just get out of your hair and let you sleep late this morning. You've been a bit grumpy the last two mornings."

Kara bit the inside of her cheek to keep herself from responding too quickly. "Well thanks. I do appreciate the extra sleep. Tell you what, I'll meet you at the zoo in an hour?"

"Oh, that won't work. Bridget has her heart set on a puppet show at 1:30. Can you meet us here instead?"

Kara winced at the thought of a puppet show with more children like Bridget. "Yeah, I'll be there soon. Just need a shower and some coffee."

"Great, Kara! Bridget will be so glad you're going to join us. See you soon!"

Kara tossed her phone back onto her bedside table and rubbed her eyes. "Lumien?"

"Good morning, Kara." Her robot's voice came through an internal earpiece, as crisp as though he was standing in front of her.

"Denise took Bridget to the carnival. Do we have any new intel on it?"

"No reports have been filed at our clearance level--a situation which would be remedied if you became an active member of the Protectorate. However, I have indications that several of the Protectorate have been running surveillance on the location for several days."

Kara toyed with the idea of calling a contact, but as she ran down the list of likely candidates, she decided that she wasn't quite ready to drag anyone else in yet. It was still hours until sunset, and the information she had gleaned about the last visit of the *Le Carnaval Pomme D'or*, mostly from the less-secure files of the Protectorate, suggested that the worst occurrences all took place after dark.

"Get my things together, Lumien. We're going to the carnival."

~

It took Kara a little longer than planned to get to the carnival. As she showered, she thought about how to explain to Denise and Bridget why they really shouldn't spend a lot of time at the carnival. She had already told Denise about the high rate of disappearances the last time the carnival came to Cobalt City. Denise, however, had chalked it up to lax parenting standards of the early 1980s. Kara bristled at the implication--she was still a few years shy of thirty, making her a child of the eighties. Denise was twelve years older than Kara, and the age difference was often apparent when they reminisced about their respective childhoods.

Kara and Lumien arrived at the carnival a little after one. Lumien had covered his brass exterior with a holographic projection of a broad-shouldered man with a toddler on each arm. Kara marveled sometimes at how good her robot was at blending in. Just as Kara was about to go over the game plan with Lumien, her cell phone rang. "Hi, Denise. Just got here."

"Oh, good! I don't know how much longer we can save you a seat at the puppet show."

"Right, puppet show." Kara scanned the map of the carnival grounds. Lumien pointed to the location on the map before she could spot it on her own. "Thanks, Lu ..." Realizing she was still connected to Denise, she cut herself off. "I'll be right there."

She hung up the phone and looked imploringly at Lumien. "Sometimes I wish that you were able to get sick. Then I'd have an excuse to get out of family visits."

Lumien looked at Kara quizzically. "Should I feign illness?"

"No, no. Just take a walk around. Try to find any hidden exits, in case we need to get out of here quickly. I'm not fond of the thought that there's only one way in or out."

"Of course, Kara."

Kara turned and headed in the direction of the puppet show. At every turn, she ignored the carnival barkers trying to lure unsuspecting patrons into their tents. Kara possessed no special way of sensing danger, but she knew that this place was giving her the creeps. In the daylight, it was the most polished carnival she had ever been to. The tents were bright and colorful, showing no signs of fading or patching. The air was heavy with scents of kettle corn and cotton candy, but without the underlying smell of vomit that usually accompanied carnival rides. By all outward appearances, this could have been one of the happiest places on earth. And that made Kara even more wary.

The only sound that caused her any alarm was the creaking of the Ferris wheel as it slowly rotated. A screech, like two pieces of metal rubbing against one another, pierced Kara's ears. She looked over toward the Ferris wheel and watched the ride operator, a hunchbacked elderly man, bang on the support beam that stabilized the ride. The screeching noise subsided as quickly as it had begun.

Reaching the puppet show, Kara bought her ticket and pushed past the heavy canvas flap of the tent. Out of the corner of her eye, she thought she saw a Chihuahua-sized creature scurry away. The dim lighting of the tent prevented her from seeing details more clearly, but she noticed a handful of soccer moms with purse dogs in the audience.

Before Kara could investigate further, Denise waved to her. Kara made her way down, moving carefully so as not to jostle any of the other patrons. She wore her leather jacket a little larger than necessary to conceal the rocket pack strapped to her back. Bumping into anyone would draw attention to the sizeable metallic mass.

"Hi, Auntie Kara," Bridget exclaimed as Kara sat down. "Aren't you excited to see the puppets?"

Kara glanced at the small puppet stage at one end of the tent. "Yeah, I'm sure it'll be really great, Bridget."

Bridget turned around and settled into her seat. Denise leaned closer to Kara. "Who's Lou?"

Kara arched one eyebrow, preparing to respond, when the audience erupted into applause. The lights in the tent dimmed, and a pair of puppets appeared on the stage, lit by the harsh white light of a single spotlight. "Saved by the puppets," she muttered.

"Oh no, you're not," Denise whispered with a sly smile.

Kara grimaced, partially at her sister and partially at the poorly piped-in music that accompanied the puppet show. The speakers distorted the sound nearly beyond recognition, but it sounded like a warped version of "Pop Goes the Weasel." Somehow, all of the children in the audience were entranced, while most of the adults in the audience were glued to their smartphones. Denise, however, focused her attention on Kara.

"What? Aren't you going to watch the puppets?" Kara asked.

"No, I want to hear about your friend, Lou."

"Lou?"

"When we were on the phone, you said 'Thanks, Lou.' So who is he? Or is it a she? Boyfriend? Girlfriend?"

Kara laughed, a far harsher sound than she had anticipated. "God, no, Denise." Then she paused, trying to figure out how to explain her robot to her sister. Lumien hadn't been out of the lab since Denise and Bridget had arrived, and Kara had simply waved past the door when she gave them the tour of her house, muttering something about the basement being a mess. "Look, can we talk about this later?"

"We're here now," Denise replied.

Kara sighed. The repetitive music was getting on her nerves, but she saw no easy escape. "Fine. Lou is short for, umm, Lucien. He's just a friend."

Denise smiled knowingly. "You say that now, but just you wait."

"You're like those people who talk in the theater, sis. Special hell. Shut up and watch the puppets."

~

Kara stood outside the puppet show tent with Denise and Bridget after the show. "So, ready for the zoo?"

"No way," Bridget said with a stomp of her foot. "Mom bought me a bunch of ride tickets. Mom, can I hold them?"

Denise dug through her purse and handed her daughter a wad of red tickets. "Put them in your pocket, honey." Bridget instead began to count the tickets, and Denise turned her attention back to Kara. "So, Lucien ..."

"Mo-oomm," Bridget interrupted. "I have fifteen ride tickets."

"Not now, honey. Auntie Kara and I are having grown-up time."

Bridget rolled her eyes, looking every bit like her mother's daughter. Kara had only been a toddler when Denise was a teenager, but she remembered her sister's attitude. She wasn't surprised that Bridget had picked it up.

"So, is he European?"

Kara laughed. "No, not exactly. Maybe a little bit Swiss, but he's not really from there."

"Swiss, huh? That sounds exotic."

"What would it take for me to convince you that Lucien and I are only friends? There's nothing there."

"Mom, I'm bored. Can I go ride the rides now?" Bridget peered up at her mother hopefully.

Denise sighed, ignoring her daughter. "Okay. But Kara, sweetie, I just think it's time for you to settle down with a nice guy. Or girl, whichever."

"Really? If I remember right, sis, that didn't work out so well for you." Kara wished she had bitten her tongue as soon as the words were out of her mouth.

Denise looked crestfallen. "You know, do as I say, not as I do. I just want you to be happy."

"I think I'm happier on my own, sis."

"I guess. But you know it would make Mom and Dad happy too. They're not as young as they once were. Mom's been talking about wanting a big Christmas again. Lots of cousins and kids running around, like it was when you were little."

Kara tried not to roll her eyes, but her arms crossed almost involuntarily as she tried to end the discussion. She turned her head away from Denise and noticed that Bridget was no longer standing near them. "Where's Bridget?"

Denise spun around, frantically looking for her daughter. Kara scanned the area more slowly, but the crowds were thick around them. Soundlessly, she channeled her thoughts into the communication system between herself and Lumien. "Lumien, Bridget has disappeared. Tell me you got that tracker implanted in her sneaker before she left?"

"Yes, it is installed and functional. Bridget appears to be approximately 20 feet above the surface of the Earth at present."

Kara shifted her gaze upward and spotted the Ferris wheel. She grabbed Denise by the arm and pointed. "She's up there."

"Bridget!" Denise exclaimed. "Why on earth would the ride operator let a seven year old on the Ferris wheel by herself?"

Kara shrugged, but Denise stalked off toward the ride, ready to give the elderly carnie a piece of her mind. Kara hung back and watched the giant wheel spin. For as new as the ride looked, the motion was not nearly as smooth as she would have expected. Brow furrowing, she pulled her goggles from an interior pocket and put them on. "Lumien, I'm sending you a feed from the Ferris wheel. Can you run it through the optics?"

"Of course, Kara." A moment passed before he spoke again. "Kara, there seems to be a growing level of energy at the center of the mechanism."

As Lumien spoke, Kara watched the wheel stop moving and shift downward. Without warning, one of the legs on either side of the Ferris wheel pulled free of the ground and began writhing, snakelike.

"The energy appears to have peaked," Lumien reported.

"I'll say. We've got trouble. I'm going to need some crowd control." Kara shrugged out of her jacket and tossed it at a nearby onlooker. "Hang on to that for me, will you?" The young man was staring at the Ferris wheel, a look of horror on his face. Kara shook her head and flipped the thrusters on her rocket pack into action.

Kara flew upwards, keeping her distance from the flailing legs of the Ferris wheel. Each broad sweep of the appendages cleared a slightly broader space, as the assembled crowds tried to run. From the air, Kara could see the likely source of the energy that had animated the Ferris wheel--the top of the axle was crackling with sickly green energy.

The caged car holding Bridget and a few other children was near the top of the Ferris wheel. Kara flew a little closer so that she could get a good look at the mechanism that held the door closed. The entire Ferris wheel shook as the free legs tugged at the two legs that were still stationary. It looked like it was trying to free itself from quicksand.

Adjusting the focus on her goggles, Kara used the zoom lens to provide a clearer view of the lock. "Lumien, I'm sending you a picture of the locking mechanism. I need to know the fastest way to get it open."

Lumien responded almost immediately. "It is an electronic bolting mechanism. A brief burst from your zap gun should disengage the lock."

Kara swooped down toward the cars that were only a few feet off the ground. "Stand clear of the door," she announced to the passengers, leveling one of her zap guns at the lock. The passengers crowded to the opposite side, and she unleashed a quick blast. The mechanism hummed, followed by a click. "Go. Get out of there and move away from the Ferris wheel." A middle-aged woman took the children by the hand and hurried out the open door.

Kara moved toward the next car, but found her way impeded by a flailing Ferris wheel leg. She rocketed upward, passing the car that Bridget was trapped in. "Aunt Kara!" The girl called out.

Kara waved at her niece dismissively. "Not now. I'm a little busy." She looked at Bridget, trying to muster up a smile. "I'll get you out of there. Promise."

As she turned her attention back to the animated ride, she spotted one of the legs flying directly toward her. She dodged to her left, her right shoulder clipping the frame of the caged car that Bridget was in. She released her hold on the zap gun in that hand, and heard it clatter off of the bars of the cage.

Before she could locate where it had fallen, the other leg swung at her, coming perilously close to the cage. "Lumien? I need help. Can you keep one of the legs occupied? I need this thing to stop swinging at me so I can get the passengers out."

"Affirmative," Lumien chirped. Kara couldn't see what her robot was up to, but one of the legs was no longer anywhere near the cages. She took off in the other direction, flying in the sorts of loops and spirals that she normally saved for paying customers who had hired her to put on an aerial show.

In the distance, Kara heard a pulse fired from her missing zap gun. She scanned the ground, trying to find it. She noticed a few small dark spots on the ground, which seemed to be heading in Lumien's direction. Before she could warn him, she saw that the door to Bridget's cage was hanging open. The girl was shimmying down one of the spokes toward the center of the Ferris wheel.

Kara cursed under her breath and started toward the thin spoke. The Ferris wheel swung at her, blocking her movement toward her niece. "Oh, now you're just making me mad." She fired off an ineffectual blast from her remaining zap gun, watching as the electricity skittered across the surface of the leg. A small shriek from Bridget was just loud enough to draw Kara's attention. The girl was still crawling down the spoke, but she waved one of her hands back and forth. Kara could just make out a scorch mark across her palm.

"Lumien, don't hit it with anything electrical. It conducts."

"Indeed," Lumien said, sounding slightly rattled. "I just received a bit of a shock myself."

"Alright, get ready. I need you to run through the center when I fly through to get Bridget. And 5, 4, 3 ..."

Before Kara could finish her countdown, she heard the swirling calliope of carnival music. She paused, watching as the wheel began to turn slowly. Bridget had reached the axle and had perched on the end of it. She fired a beam of electricity downward, aiming for a gap in the loading platform. Two of the cages moved onto the loading platform, and Bridget stopped.

Kara grinned from ear to ear, and fired off two quick shots to unlock the doors of the cars. Bridget turned her head slightly, and Kara could see that the girl's facial expression matched hers.

"Scratch that, Lumien. Just keep the thing distracted while we get the passengers out."

Bridget continued to rotate the Ferris wheel to move more occupied cars into the unloading position. Kara began flying long, lazy ellipsoid shapes to keep the animated Ferris wheel occupied and get herself into the right position to unlock the doors as soon as Bridget had cars in position. The two of them made quick work of the job, and Kara flew up toward her niece.

"Not bad, kiddo. Now let's get you out of here." She stretched out her arms to the girl.

"Aunt Kara, watch out!" Bridget exclaimed. Too late, Kara turned to see one of the legs plow into her midsection. As the air escaped her lungs, the rocket pack sputtered, threatening to stall. She regained enough of her senses to steer herself toward a nearby tent, but the impact was nearly as bad as it would have been had she hit the ground.

"Lumien?" she croaked.

"I am having a bit of unanticipated difficulty at the moment, Kara. I will get to you as soon as I can."

"Unanticipated difficulty?"

"Yes, Kara. At the moment, there are puppets attached to all of my appendages. They have drained my power capacity to less than 40 percent."

"I guess jolting them isn't an option then." She thought for a moment, lifting herself up on her elbows to survey the scene. Bridget clutched the axle as tightly as she could while staying away from the strange energy there. Lumien was, as he said, covered in small dark shapes that looked a lot like the thing Kara had spotted earlier at the puppet show. "Wait. Get as close to the Ferris wheel as you can. It's got way more power than you do. Get the puppets to attack it!"

Lumien's voice sounded tired, like a record played too slowly. "Yes, Kara."

Kara braced herself and rose to her knees. Every inch of her body hurt, but she had enough self-control to pilot the rocket pack. She hoped she would have enough strength to safely transport her niece to the ground. Falling would not be an option with a seven year old girl clinging to her.

She watched as Lumien wrapped his arms around the remaining leg on his side of the Ferris wheel. Instantly, the puppets released their hold on him and began scurrying up toward the axle. Kara activated her rocket pack and flew toward Bridget.

"Bridget, you crawled down that spoke and didn't fall. I need you to hold on to me just as tight."

Bridget nodded solemnly, tucking the zap gun back into the holster on Kara's chest. She slung her arms around Kara's neck and squeezed her knees around Kara's hips. One of the Ferris wheel's legs flailed in their direction, but fell short. Kara still didn't want to take any chances. She flew away from the Ferris wheel twice as far as the legs could reach and landed, carefully lowering Bridget to the ground.

"Is your robot going to be okay?" Bridget asked.

"How did you ... oh, I guess he can't hide himself right now. He'll be fine." Kara glanced up and noticed Denise rushing in their direction. "Here comes your mom."

"Bridget! Kara!" Denise exclaimed. "Are you alright?"

"We're fine, Mom," Bridget replied. "Aren't we, Aunt Kara?"

"Thanks to you," Kara admitted. She looked at Denise. "You've got yourself a little Sparx, that's for sure."

"Unexpected Sparx" first appeared in Cobalt City Dark Carnival.

BIG IN JAPAN

Kara Sparx held her breath, her mouth a tight line, as she pulled the trigger on her newest invention. For a moment, there was no outward effect. Then the air about ten feet ahead of her shimmered. The corners of her lips twitched upward as the shimmering spot widened, resolving itself into a wavy-edged portal, rimmed with glowing green light.

Behind her, Snowflake gasped. His words came out in a near blur. "Oh god you made a portal gun that works!" His stubby fingers twitched. "Can I hold it?"

Kara pulled the gun up and close to her body. Snowflake was her friend, but the uplifted panda was known for his inappropriate love of guns. "Better if you don't. It's still in the testing phase."

"Okay, fine. So where's the other end?"

Kara shrugged. "It's not exactly like the video game."

"Yeah, but it still goes somewhere, right?"

"Well, yes, that's the whole point. It's just like the portals you told me about, with the warlord panda you and the scientist panda you. They're just generated with my gun instead of the tech you couldn't be bothered to remember well enough to tell me about."

"Hey, I was busy trying not to get killed by the warlord panda me. He had my undivided attention. So which iteration does it go to?"

"I don't know." Kara peered through the portal. On the other side were squat wooden frame cottages with sliding doors and thatched roofs. They reminded her of Japanese homes she had seen in the movies, but with small differences. Every house had a chimney that billowed smoke that looked more like steam, which Kara pinpointed as the likely source of the lingering fog that hung over the entire area. A few tendrils of fog slithered through the portal, bringing with them the chill of this other iteration.

Kara frowned. "When you saw the other portals, your counterpart was right on the other side, right?"

"Yeah. I guess they were both looking for me. Well, Warlord Xuĕhuā was looking for Doctor Xuĕhuā to destroy him, and then Doctor Xuĕhuā was looking for me to make sure Warlord Xuĕhuā didn't destroy me."

Kara waved her hand at Snowflake. "Right, it's complicated?"

"It *is* complicated. Have you ever had an evil version of yourself try to kill you? Naming conventions get weird."

"I'll have to take your word on it." Kara turned back to the portal. "But I don't see any version of me over there."

"So let's go looking!"

Before she responded, a fierce wind whipped through the portal, rustling the blueprint Kara had left on one of her workbenches. "Grab that!" she shouted.

Snowflake lunged toward the blueprint, but the wind shifted and pulled the paper just out of his grasp and through the portal.

"No, don't!" Kara exclaimed as he moved toward the entry. "We don't know anything about that iteration!"

"We know your top secret plan is over there now, and scooting down the street." He peered into the portal. "They've got some strange weather there, that's for sure."

Kara sighed and joined Snowflake at the portal. Her blueprint skittered along, almost as though it had grown legs and was running away from her. "How is it that you can be so clumsy, and yet a good pilot?"

"I have specialized skills, alright?"

Kara set the portal gun on the worktable and picked up a grappling gun. It wasn't designed for fine motor control, but she'd used it like a fishing pole before. She aimed and pulled the trigger.

The grappling hook shot out from the gun and landed square atop the blueprint, slowing its movement away from her. Kara flipped the switch to the slow retrieval setting. As she did, Snowflake jostled her, his stubby panda fingers grabbing at the portal gun. Kara lurched forward, helped along by another gust of wind from the portal. The combination knocked her off her feet, and she fell through the portal and hurtled toward the cobbled pavement and her blueprint.

She grabbed for the controls for her jetpack before realizing the jetpack was back in the lab. All that was left to do was to brace for impact. She tucked her arms and legs tight to her body, and shielded her face.

The uneven surface knocked the wind out of her, but she managed to roll with the impact rather than skidding across the ground. She had landed inches away from the blueprints, and grabbed them.

A wave of vertigo washed over her as she rose and turned around. A faint pinkish-purple rimmed ring hung in the air. Through it, the clean white tiled floor of her lab was visible, her workspaces spread out beyond. And Snowflake, picking up the portal gun.

"No!" she shouted. Snowflake's gaze was fixed on the gun, eyes wide with wonder. Kara ran toward the portal, but it was already too late. Snowflake was in profile from her perspective, the gun aimed at one of the other walls. She watched him fumble with the trigger. Almost immediately, the edges of the pinkish-purple portal began to collapse in on themselves, and the gap between the worlds dwindled down to a pinprick before it disappeared.

Kara switched on her communicator. "Snowflake, you monumental klutz!" she bellowed. She waited, hoping he was too busy contemplating his idiocy to make it over to the old speaker box in the lab. She kept the channel open, but also connected another channel directly to Lumien. "Lumien, are you there?"

The silence that followed was unexpected. Normally, her robot would have chirped back "Affirmative." His lack of response meant she had lost communication with her home iteration.

She tried to pull up her heads-up display, but the image flickered for an instant and then dimmed, not even fully resolving. "Damn," she muttered. Without any of her usual tech, she was at a loss. "Alright, Sparx. Time to find ... whatever passes for you in this place?"

Rolling up the blueprints, she looked around at the village houses. All of them were about the same size, with little individuality evident in any of their designs. She wasn't sure where she expected her counterpart to live, but none of these houses seemed quite right.

As she contemplated where to start going door to door to ask after herself, the door to one of the houses opened, and two women emerged. The first paused to raise a paper parasol. She wore a gingham print kimono, pale blue and white, her dark hair styled in an elaborate pile of knots and twists atop her head.

The woman behind her looked younger, but her hair and dress were similar, though her kimono was a pink and gray chevron pattern. Or, rather, the top half of her kimono. The woman's legs, from at least the knees down, were encased in a gleaming metal exoskeleton that helped her teeter down the narrow stairs in front of the house.

Kara approached the two women, curious enough about the younger woman's legs to forget her manners. Just before Kara got too close, she remembered herself and smiled at both of the women. The younger woman's eyes grew wide, and she bowed her head, averting her gaze from Kara. The older woman straightened for a moment, but then assumed the same posture as the younger woman.

"Um, hello, I'm looking for someone who looks like me?" Neither woman responded. "Okay, so maybe I'm called Warlord Sparx, or Doctor Sparx?"

"Supāku-sensei," the younger woman said softly.

Kara tilted her head to the side. "Spark-u?"

"Supāku-sensei," the older woman repeated. She squinted at Kara. *"Anata wa kanojode wa arimasen?"*

Kara sighed. "Lumien? I need a translator." Silence continued on both of the channels she had open. She sighed again and turned her attention back to the women. "Can you show me Spark-u sensei?" She gestured at her eyes, then pointed at herself as she spoke.

The older woman nodded, and repeated Kara's gestures. *"Supāku-sensei."*

Kara shook her head. "Not Spark-u sensei." She laid one palm flat and walked two fingers across it. "I am a traveler." Then she moved her hand to above her eyes. "I'm looking for Spark-u sensei."

The younger woman leaned forward and whispered something to the older, and the older woman's eyes widened. *"Supāku-sensei,"* she repeated, but this time, she pointed into the distance.

Kara followed the woman's gesture toward a dark colored spot in the fog. As she looked more closely, she identified curved dark eaves at several elevations, separated by pale blue strips dotted with darkened windows. Though it was high atop one of the nearby hills, it looked like a large pagoda. A smile spread across her face. "Yes," she said. "Thank you." She stammered for a moment. "Uh, *arigato*?"

The women smiled and nodded, both giving repeated shallow bows as she walked away from them. "Note to self," Kara muttered under her breath. "Learn to speak something other than English before I get yanked into the next iteration I find."

~

The hill the pagoda was perched atop was missing chunks. Kara wished she had her jetpack, so she could fly up and examine the gaps. But from the ground, it appeared that the edges of the holes were blackened in places, probably from explosions. The fact that these missing spots were along the main road that led up the hill was of more concern.

Kara looked at a nearby tree and hefted her grappling gun. She shot up into the branches, and tugged to make sure the line was secure. Then she flipped the switch to pull her toward the branch. As soon as it was in reach, she grabbed the branch with her other hand, and swung herself up onto it. From the higher vantage point, she saw other impacts to the surface of the hill, these shaped more like fist imprints, but the size of a small car. Kara frowned. "Lumien, I need your eyes," she muttered to herself. "We've gotta work on communicating across dimensions."

As she unwound the grappling hook from the tree branch and tucked it back into her belt, her fingers brushed across the lens of one of her pairs of goggles. The magnification was far inferior to Lumien's optics, but it was better than nothing. She pulled them on and fiddled with the settings until the hillside was clear in her field of vision.

Three flying insectoid constructs, each the size of a housecat and made of a shimmering reflective metal, hovered into Kara's view. They were nearer to the hill than to her, but headed in her direction. She made a quick mental inventory of what she might have with her, but the grappling gun and the blue prints were the only things that came to mind. She patted her pockets, hopeful she had forgotten about another one of her inventions, but came up with nothing more.

She scooted back on the branch to lean against the tree trunk, and she crossed her ankles to keep herself stably seated on the tree branch. She drew her grappling gun and sighted across the top of it at the flying bugs, hoping, at the very least, they would be startled by the grappling hook.

Before she had a chance to find out, the trio of insects paused mid-air. The one at the front twitched, and a small compartment on its back opened, from which a device emerged that reminded Kara of her early zap gun design.

Frowning, she tried to reproduce the name the two women in the village had repeated. "Spark-u sensei?"

A tinny voice emanated from one of the insects, but the words were impossible for Kara to identify.

She tried again. "I'm looking for someone who calls herself Spark-u sensei."

A pause followed. "Doctor Sparx? I thought you were in your lab." The voice sounded like Lumien's, though the inflection was different.

"I'm not Doctor Sparx," Kara said. "My name is Kara Sparx. I think I'm looking for this Doctor Sparx, though."

"Ah, then I advise you to fly up to the pagoda."

"Uh, I can't fly."

Another pause. "The flyers register your position some meters above the surface of the earth."

Kara chuckled. "I'm in a tree."

"Oh. Never fear, the flyers can accommodate your mass. Do not be alarmed. They will approach you now, and bring you to meet Doctor Sparx."

As the voice continued, the three flyers flew toward Kara, the leader retracting his weapon before he reached her. One flyer went to each of her arms, while the third flew behind her. Slender metal limbs wrapped around both of her forearms and tugged, while the other spread across her back and shoulders. She uncrossed her ankles, and the insects lifted her out of the tree in smooth unison.

~

The pagoda was more impressive up close. What had looked like a simple pale blue from the ground was a reflective metal, much like that from which the flyers were constructed. At this angle, the pagoda exterior reflected the tall, slender gingko trees that dotted the hillside. Although the camouflage effect was imperfect on the whole, some portions of the pagoda blended in with their surroundings, making it look much smaller than it was.

An elderly Japanese man stood in the doorway as the flyers set Kara back down. He glanced back inside, and then looked at Kara. "You are not Doctor Sparx?"

"Nope, never got a doctorate. And you are?"

"Akihiko." He gave a deep bow. "Follow me."

As Kara followed Akihiko through the pagoda, a flock of household servants peeked out from various hallways and doorways, all whispering to each other as she passed. She tried to ignore them and focus on the décor, but found it difficult. She was not accustomed to so many people around--at home, it was just her and Lumien, and he gave new meaning to the word unobtrusive.

At the end of the hallway, huge double doors parted. Akihiko stopped just before he reached the threshold and gestured within. "You'll find her here."

"Thanks, Akihiko. Does she know to expect me?"

He nodded, a small smile playing across his lips. "Of course she does."

Kara smiled nervously and stepped into the lab space. The same cold wind that had pulled her blueprints into the portal ruffled her hair. One end of the lab space was open to the sky beyond. Along the edges of the room stood giant robots, their bowed heads nearly at the towering ceiling. A few smaller models were interspersed between the giants, but even the smaller ones were at least 100 feet tall. Work crews clambered over the surface of the mechas like ants swarming over the remains of a picnic. And in the center of the room stood a woman who Kara could not fail to recognize-- Doctor Sparx.

Despite the clear Japanese origin of everything else around, Doctor Sparx did not appear to be Japanese. She had the same brown hair and brown eyes that Kara had, though her hair was long and bound up in elaborate knots like the women in the village. Her clothes were far more utilitarian, drab browns and greens, with snug slacks and a straight-sleeved short wool jacket.

Doctor Sparx inclined her head to the side, but smiled as she approached Kara. "Akihiko said you speak English, so hello."

"Hi," Kara replied. She gestured at the robots lining the room. "Did you build all of these?"

"Build? Not personally. But I designed them."

"They're magnificent!"

"Thank you. But I think you did not come here just to see my mecha."

"No, in fact, if I had been a little more careful, I wouldn't be here at all. I built a portal gun, and then the wind took my blueprints, and when I tried to get them back, I fell in."

Doctor Sparx frowned. "Why would you use a gun to make a portal?"

"Oh, it's a ... a thing from my home iteration." Kara shrugged. "And it seemed like a good idea at the time?"

"I see." Though Doctor Sparx didn't betray any outward signs, Kara knew her counterpart was silently judging her. "And the portal you made?"

"Got closed when Snowflake ..." Kara paused and looked around. "You don't have a giant man-panda running around here, do you?"

Doctor Sparx arched her eyebrow, but shook her head. "Perhaps in the Qing States, to the southwest, but there are no pandas here."

Kara sighed with relief, but then frowned. "Wait, where is here?"

"Hiizurukuni. Or Iteration 8102482. And you are from?"

"Um, Cobalt City, Massachusetts, United States, Earth? I don't know the iteration number."

"No?" Doctor Sparx arched her eyebrow again, and Kara found herself wanting to practice that expression. It looked very impressive. "How did you get here then?"

"Accident, really," Kara admitted. "I just wanted to see if I could build a gun that made portals to other places. I haven't had much of a chance to test it out yet, but I think it's safe to say it just finds an alternate iteration."

Doctor Sparx blinked a few times, mouth agape. She had gone beyond judging Kara to outright shock. "Well, at least I suppose you had no intentions of rushing headlong into the first iteration you found, so there's that," she said, after several long moments of staring at Kara. "Now then." Doctor Sparx chewed at her thumb.

Kara chuckled.

"What?" Doctor Sparx asked.

"I do the same thing when I'm thinking."

Doctor Sparx chuckled in response. "If you can give me a sample of your hair, and maybe some loose fibers from your clothes, I should be able to help you find your way back home."

Kara reached up to pluck a strand of hair, but before she could, an enormous booming sound filled the mecha hangar.

"Damn," Doctor Sparx muttered.

"What in the world is that?"

"Danshaku Sandā ... ah, he's a nobleman who owns much of the surrounding countryside."

"Does he often knock so loudly?"

"Always. He's asked for my hand in marriage, but I'm not interested."

Kara smiled. "So why don't you just blast him with your mecha?"

"Alas, he has twice the number I've been able to construct, and they're larger and more powerful than mine. I came to this place to learn to build mecha from scientists like him, but he has decided he would rather have me as an ornament than a scientific comrade. Were you seen in the village?"

"Yes, by a couple of women who pointed me in your direction."

"He probably believes I went out walking alone. He's been hounding me to allow him to accompany me on a walk for months."

Before she could continue, the ground trembled beneath them, causing Kara to stumble. Doctor Sparx dropped into a low crouch, more accustomed to what Kara guessed were assaults on the hillside.

Kara regained her footing and scanned the mecha. "More and tougher, eh? How would they deal with something small and quick? How many does it take to pilot a mecha?"

"Ten for the *kyodai*--the large ones--at least three for the small. What do you plan to do, Kara Sparx?"

"I was thinking of dissuading your suitor for a little while, if that's alright with you." She tugged out a few strands of hair and shrugged out of her jacket, handing both to Doctor Sparx. "How

45

long do you need to calculate how to send me home?"

~

Kara's nose itched, but she dared not reach to scratch it. A series of leather straps and brass contacts connected the motion of her arms to that of the mecha she was helping to pilot, one that Doctor Sparx called Terasu. When the inventor had explained that it translated to "illuminate," Kara had picked it as the one she wanted to pilot. "I've gotta make me one of these."

"Kara-*san*?" One of the two assistant pilots looked up at her from her perch in the left leg.

"Are we ready, Keiko?"

The young woman blushed. "We are, Kara-*san*, but I am Erina."

"Sorry, Erina on the left, Keiko on the right. And all I need to do is run the weapons systems?"

"*Hai*," Erina replied with a nod. "We'll handle the flight functions from here."

"Alright, then let's go!"

Erina and Keiko both grasped the controls in front of them and began shouting in a staggered pattern--first Erina, then Keiko. As they did, the mecha moved forward--first the left foot, then the right. The mecha's feet pounded across the steel floor of the hangar, and Kara watched as the wide opening grew larger and larger in her view screen. Soon, the hangar floor was gone, and a moment later, the mecha dropped several feet down. Before she could even blink, the thrusters kicked in, and the mecha took flight.

"Tuck your arms!" Erina shouted. Kara did as she was instructed, careful to keep her fingers extended and together, as the young women had taught her. Her every gesture translated to movement in the mecha's upper half, and precision was key to not blasting Doctor Sparx's pagoda. Or the hill that held it in place.

"Can we get higher?"

"*Hai*," Keiko replied, and the mecha responded.

As they ascended, Kara spotted Danshaku Sandā's force arrayed around the hill. A dozen mecha, far bigger than Doctor Sparx's largest units, were positioned at the foot of the hill, surrounding it on every side.

"Command reports ten minutes to scramble our full force, Kara-*san*," Keiko said, her voice wavering.

"Okay, we can handle this. We have more maneuverability than them, right?"

"Hai," Erina replied. "We have three times their speed."

"But they have at least twice our firepower," Keiko whispered, just loud enough for Kara to hear.

"Then we don't let them hit us." Kara double checked the positioning. "The three mecha in the northwest quadrant of the hill are nearer to each other than the others. We start there. Get as close to them as we can, as low to the ground as you can."

The two young women nodded, and the faintest glimmer of a smile appeared on Erina's face. She called out something in rapid fire Japanese, and Keiko responded with a nod.

"Diver arms!" Erina called out, and Kara complied. The mecha sped up, and Kara had a terrifying view of the ginkgo trees and the ground beneath them as they plummeted toward it.

When they reached the northwest quadrant, Terasu began weaving back and forth around the three mecha, once even slipping between the legs of one of the mecha. The visuals were dizzying, but Kara stared straight ahead, watching for an opening.

As Terasu arced out to one side, preparing for another run, Kara saw her opportunity. She clenched both her fists and stretched her arms above her head. Bright golden bolts shot out from either side of her viewscreen and pummeled the back of the enemy mecha's knees. Terasu flew backward from the momentum of the shot. "Yeah!" Kara shouted.

Her elation was short lived. The mecha's knees did not buckle, and it did not pitch forward into the nearest mecha. Its stance did not even waver, despite the charred patches across the back of its legs.

"Their armor ..." Keiko began.

"Let me guess, at least as twice as good as ours?"

"Four times." Keiko tilted her head to one side and mouthed what Kara guessed were numbers, as though she was calculating. "Oh, perhaps only twice as strong on the back of the knees."

"Take us back up high," Kara said. As the mecha rose, she asked "Do they have any weak spots?"

"If they do, we have not found them yet," Keiko replied.

"Okay, how do you normally get rid of them, then?"

"The *kyodai* ... ah, the giant mecha. They have increased firepower. A few shots from the *kyodai* will usually cause Danshaku

Sandā to retreat."

"So what do we do for ten minutes?"

Erina and Keiko were separated by at least two layers of thick metal plating--the inner walls of each leg--but from Kara's perspective, they turned to face each other and smiled. "We sting like mosquitos," they said in unison.

Kara laughed. "Alright, that sounds like a plan I can handle."

The two pilots maneuvered Terasu back into the fray, darting between the enemy mecha with skill. When Kara saw openings, she took shots, hoping to at least damage Danshaku Sandā's force, even if they could not destroy it. One of her shots hit a mecha in the face, and it staggered backward.

"Look out!" she shouted as Terasu twirled into the spot where the stumbling mecha was about to plant its foot. The screech of metal on metal pierced Kara's ears, and she fought the urge to cover her ears with her hands, knowing Terasu would make the same motion. Terasu continued to move, but its momentum slowed. She looked down at the two pilots. A veil of sparks prevented her from seeing Erina.

"Are you alright?" she shouted. Something pale and small waved from somewhere in the left leg. "Keiko, left leg is hit. We need to get out of here."

"Hai," Keiko said. "Mecha Terasu, returning to hangar."

"Negative," a voice Kara didn't recognize responded across the comm channel. "We have incoming at the hangar. Repeat, do not approach the hangar."

Kara looked down at Keiko, her eyes widening. "Is that one of Doctor Sparx's people?"

Keiko nodded, her eyes matching Kara's.

"Then where ..." Kara's voice trailed off.

Keiko looked back at her screens and fumbled with the controls. "Vertical thrust is at 30 percent. Horizontal thrust is at 47 percent and dropping." She looked back up. "Is Erina ..."

"I'm okay," Erina said. "But I need to come up now." She flipped a switch in her control panel and looked up expectantly.

Kara followed Erina's gaze to a panel on the ceiling of the cockpit. "What's up there?"

"We have ladders to get out of the legs that descend from above. But the hatch must be jammed." Erina toggled the switch, but then looked up at Kara and shook her head.

"I've got a grappling gun in my holster, will that help?"

Erina sucked in a sharp breath. "It's on your left hip. If you reach for it, you may knock the left leg loose." She went silent for a moment. "I can try to climb out."

"Be careful," Keiko wailed.

"Hang on, I've got an idea," Kara said. She bit the collar of her shirt and jerked her head backward. The fabric slid out from under her belt, but it moved the hip holster over her left leg. She raised her leg, pushing up on the bottom of the holster until the grappling gun started to move upward and out of the holster.

Just as she had gotten it clear of the holster, Terasu shuddered, and the gun clattered to the floor. The mecha slid backward, and Kara's shoulders burned as the straps kept her arms locked into place while her body tried to slide away.

"What was that?" she cried out.

"We're caught," Keiko said, eyes glued to Kara's display screen.

Kara looked up at the screen, noticing her grappling gun lying far out of her reach. The sky pitched, and then jolted as an enemy mecha lifted Terasu up to face level.

"Keiko, can you get to the grappling gun?"

Keiko glanced up over the edge of her cockpit. "If I do, we won't be able to go anywhere."

"Leave that to me. Get the gun, and get Erina out of her leg."

Keiko nodded, and Kara turned her attention back to the enemy mecha in front of them. She pulled her arms down into the tucked resting position.

"Do you surrender?" Lights danced across the mouth of the mecha in time with its tinny voice.

Kara hesitated, sparing a quick glance down at Keiko, who stood at the top of Terasu's left leg. Erina's head poked up over the edge, and scrabbled at the floor beneath Kara. She looked at the other mecha, and arched her eyebrow, even though she knew Terasu's face would not match hers.

"If you think I'm here to surrender, you don't know much about the Sparx." She thrust both of her arms forward, hands forming into fists and punching, unleashing a massive blast into the mecha's face at short range. The force of the blast loosed Terasu from the enemy mecha's grasp, and Doctor Sparx's creation hurtled backward.

"Up, up, up," she shouted as they flew. Keiko and Erina both clambered into the right leg, and in an instant, Terasu's backward motion had been converted into a decidedly right-leaning upward motion.

The mecha slowed as they rose from the ground, but Kara continued her chant beneath her breath. She realigned her arms so her fists faced the ground, and loosed a quick blast, supplementing the ailing vertical thrusters with the backward momentum the weapons system provided. Terasu ascended out of the reach of the mechas on the ground, but the enemy mechas fired up thrusters of their own.

Before any of them rose far, a shadow flickered across Kara's viewscreen, and one of Doctor Sparx's *kyodai* interposed itself between Terasu and the mechas on the ground.

"Rucksack," Erina called out.

Kara reminded herself not to flail her arms. "Uh, we didn't practice that one."

"Be his rucksack!"

Realization dawned on Kara, and she slung her arms forward, draping Terasu's arms over the larger mecha's shoulders and then grasping her left wrist with her right hand. The pilots released the controls, and the *kyodai* fired its thrusters, lifting Terasu and its pilots to safety.

~

Kara climbed down from Terasu, giving the mecha one last pat as she did. She glanced at the mechanics who had already surrounded the damaged leg. "Sorry about that," she said.

"We can rebuild him," one of them said.

"Make him better, stronger, and faster, okay?"

Kara looked around the now half-empty hangar for Doctor Sparx. She saw the portal first--green at the edges, just like the one in her lab, but Doctor Sparx's portal was circular rather than oblong. Kara hurried over.

Through the portal, she saw Snowflake and Lumien. No sound came through, but based on Snowflake's wild gestures and moving mouth, he was panicking. Lumien's face was not articulated to show outward emotion, but Kara could read the pulsing patterns of his single glowing eye well enough--if he were human, he'd be about one breath away from hyperventilating. Neither of them looked in the direction of the portal, even when she waved.

"Can they not see us?"

Doctor Sparx gestured to a large plate made of the same reflective surface as her flyers positioned opposite the portal opening. "If you have sensors in your lab that detect dimensional activity, they have been triggered. But I find it useful to conceal when I am looking in on another iteration, at least at first."

An explosion rocked the hangar, and Kara looked at Doctor Sparx. "You know, you don't have to stay here. You could come back to Cobalt City. We have far fewer angry warlords hellbent on marriage there."

"Thank you for the offer, but I've made this my home. These people rely on me to keep them safe. Besides," she paused, looking through the portal. "I am not fond of panda men."

"Sometimes, I feel that way too," Kara murmured, watching Snowflake through the slight distortion that the portal created. Then a thought struck her. "The mecha I flew didn't have very good visual range. Is that true for all of them?"

"Yes, I haven't had time to fix the optics yet."

"What about sensors?"

"Rudimentary at best. The technology doesn't exist here to support it."

"So would the same be true of Danshaku Sandā's mecha?"

Doctor Sparx blushed at that. "Well, unless he's made vast strides since he developed the design."

Kara paused, arching her eyebrow. "You stole the design from him?"

"Ah ... elements of the design, yes. To be fair, some of them were collaborative."

"Wait, you worked with him?"

"Yes, for a time. His marriage proposal was, I believe, an attempt to push me out of the field. I declined and ended our work together. That's when the armament race started."

Kara frowned, deep in thought. "Aside from you accepting his proposal, what would it take to end this?"

"I'd need far more mecha than I have the capacity to construct in this space."

"That, I can help you with," Kara said, her frown turning into a wide smile. "If they've got bad optics, and no sensors, I'm not going to have to do much work at all. But I will need to go back to my lab for a few things."

"I thought you were anxious to return home."

"I am. But I'm not going to leave my counterpart trapped in a situation that might lead her to marry her scientific rival." Kara shuddered. "No, I've got a plan. I just need my science team."

Kara poked her head through the portal. Klaxons assaulted her ears, and she shouted to be heard. "Hey, guys, it's me, coming through."

Snowflake shrieked, dropping the portal gun to the floor. Kara winced, hoping it wouldn't trigger a new portal when it clattered against the tiles.

"Oh god, Kara, you're alive! I thought you'd die of dysentery while you were trapped in some low-tech place!"

"Dysentery?"

"It could happen," Snowflake insisted.

Kara looked back over her shoulder. Doctor Sparx's portal blended almost seamlessly with the wall behind her. "The sensors went off because an unknown portal opened."

"Yeah, but we couldn't see it, and we couldn't tell if it would be you, or evil mad scientist you, or maybe even the nuthouse you!"

"Nuthouse?" Kara looked at Lumien.

"It is a long story, Kara, one that I am certain Snowflake will tell you, at length. In the meantime, welcome home."

"Thanks, but I'm just popping back for some tools. And some help." She started to collect the equipment she needed, then paused. "Hey, Snowflake, ever wanted to fly a mecha?"

~

The inside of the smaller mechas had not been designed with a panda and a hologram-projecting robot as part of the crew. Lumien had no complaints about being strapped to the wall of the cockpit, but Snowflake had more to say about his predicament.

"These straps are chafing everything, Kara. I mean *everything*."

"I don't want to hear about it, Snowflake."

"Everything!"

"If you want to fly the mecha, you're going to have to suck it up."

Snowflake grumbled under his breath, but turned his attention back to Keiko, who was reviewing the arm controls with him.

"Kara?" Doctor Sparx's voice came over the cockpit speakers. "We're sustaining heavy damage in the east quadrant. How much longer will it be before you can get back out there?"

"I haven't had a chance to get Lumien's array up yet. But I think everyone else is ready." She looked at Keiko and Erina. "How long can you keep Sandā's mecha off of us?"

The girls looked at each other, and then to Snowflake. "If we fly high, and take long range shots, we can manage 10 minutes?" Keiko suggested.

"Assuming they don't see what we're doing and target us," Erina added.

Snowflake smiled, which was terrifying on his ursine face. "Don't worry, ladies. We'll be a ninja mecha. Hiyah!"

Kara tapped the button to respond to Doctor Sparx. "Alright, we'll get out there. Divert some of the *kyodai* to defend that area, and we'll fill in the gaps they leave."

Kara fastened her own harness around her waist and shoulders and clipped the tether line to a loop on the wall near Lumien.

"Kara, I have already done fifty-seven percent of the work necessary to use this machine as a transmitter," Lumien chirped.

"Great, a head start." The mecha shuddered as it took flight. "I think we're going to need all the time we can get."

Kara clung to the handholds on the wall at first, but Snowflake was a quick learner, even in an unfamiliar craft. With Keiko and Erina's help, the mecha flew even more smoothly than Kara had managed. She unwound her grip from the handholds and tapped open the panel that was Lumien's chest.

The orderly circuit boards within further calmed Kara, even when the mecha lurched to one side. "Ow," Snowflake said, though it didn't sound like he was in actual pain. "Time to give them back a little taste of what we've got." The panda brought both hands forward and thrust his fists in the same direction. The mecha shot backward even as bright beams blasted out of its palms. "Firepower and reverse propulsion? I love it!" Snowflake cackled.

Kara clipped long wires to parts of Lumien's holographic array, and then looked across the cockpit. Though the mecha didn't have the sort of visual amplification capabilities she was accustomed to, she had a plan. She twirled one of the devices she used for her light shows in Cobalt City until she found the port she wanted, and then plugged in the opposite end of the wire.

"Snowflake, I need you to hold level long enough for me to get to the pulse generator."

"Uh, define level," he said as the mecha jigged to one side."

"The opposite of that. I need to run from here to over there." Kara gestured with her free hand. "I'd rather not land on either of the leg pilots."

"Shoulda brought your jetpack."

"I don't fly indoors."

"Guess you didn't think that one through. I'll do what I can."

"Kara, I have analyzed the attack patterns," Lumien said. "If we fly up another 100 meters, we should be out of range of the machines on the ground."

"Snowflake," Kara began.

"On it, boss." Snowflake dropped his arms to his sides and clenched his fists. "Up!"

The mecha flew straight up, and Kara unclipped her tether line from the wall. Crouching low, she made her way across the cockpit.

"Incoming?" Snowflake said. "Hey, nobody told me they can fly too!"

"*Hai,*" Keiko said. Her face grew pale. "But they are not usually so agile."

"Kara-*san*, hold on!" Erina shouted. "Snowflake-*san*, roll!"

Kara scrambled to grab another handhold and clutched the amplification device to her chest. Her arm burned as the mecha spun and what had been the front of the cockpit became up. A moment later, she slammed into the wall as up became down.

As soon as the rotation slowed, Kara released the loop and ran for the control panel she needed. The door wouldn't budge when she grabbed it. She tucked the device under her arm to free up her other hand.

Before she could tug open the panel, the mecha dropped, and she lost her footing. She tucked her limbs around the device to cradle it as she crashed to the floor, narrowly missing falling into the leg that Keiko piloted.

The mecha leveled, and Kara stood shakily. "Are we okay?"

"Fine," Snowflake replied. Both of the other pilots called out, "*Hai!*"

"Lumien?"

"The wire has disconnected," he said. Kara turned back toward him. The end of the wire lay about a meter away from Lumien's feet. Strapped to the wall as he was, it was even out of the reach of his long arms.

Kara sighed. "Okay, I'll hook this up over here, and find some way to strap it in, and then I'll come back over and reconnect it." She shook her head. "I need another me."

"Yeah, but you left her back in the pagoda," Snowflake said.

Kara wrenched open the cover for the pulse generator. She smiled at the neat rows of circuits, glad her counterpart seemed to share the same love of order in her work. She found the appropriate port and connected the amplification device. "Snowflake, don't fire again until I give you the word."

"Okay, but ... what do you want me to do if there's a mecha coming our direction?"

Kara looked up at the viewscreen. One of Danshaku Sandā's mechas flew directly toward them. "Evade." Kara said, sweat breaking out on her face. "You have to evade."

Though Kara had never before today thought mechas existed outside of the movies and anime, she had seen enough of both to understand that the incoming mecha was on a collision trajectory. And it had double the mass of Terasu. If it hit them, they were doomed.

"Left leg offline!" Erina called out. In a blur of motion, she clambered out of her leg of the mecha and grabbed the loose end of the cord. Meanwhile, Keiko doubled her activity, and the mecha began to jerkily fly to the right. Snowflake leaned in the same direction, arms bent at the elbows and pulled in close to his torso. The scream of metal drowned out whatever Lumien said to Erina as she reached toward his open chest compartment. But a beep from Kara's amplification device told her all she needed to know.

"Snowflake, fire! Aim anywhere but at that mecha!"

Snowflake frowned, but stretched both arms out to the sides and growled, clenching and unclenching his fists as he did.

Kara clung to the wall and stared up at the viewscreen. Snowflake's shots were suitably misdirected. Where they would have reached the limit of their range, they exploded in a shower of golden sparks that then coalesced into a shimmering *kyodai*. To Kara's practiced eye, they looked two-dimensional--not her best work.

But the effect was quick. Danshaku Sandā's mechas fell back. Kara watched the mecha's energy levels, and shouted, "Keep firing!

Put some in the space between us!"

"I never thought missing my target could be this much fun!" Snowflake bellowed.

Kara looked down at Keiko. "Want some help getting back to the hangar?"

"Soon," the girl murmured. "But first I want to watch those mecha run."

~

"Kara, you don't understand," Snowflake said as he, Kara, and Lumien stood looking at Doctor Sparx's fleet of mechas. "We *need* mechas in Cobalt City. What happens when the *kaiju* attack? You're our only hope."

"I don't think Stardust would be too thrilled with me manufacturing an army for the defense of Cobalt City. I mean, that is sort of his gig."

"Yeah, but there's only one Stardust. You could make like ten mechas. Or, you know what, I'm reasonable. Maybe we'd only need five."

"Tell you what, Snowflake. If the *kaiju* attack Cobalt City, then Doctor Sparx and I will figure out a way to enlarge the portal enough so we can bring her mecha through. Deal?"

Snowflake sighed. "Fine. Ruin my fun." He looked at Doctor Sparx. "Or I could come over here and fly your mecha for funsies?"

Doctor Sparx blinked at Snowflake. "Funsies? No, I think not. I appreciate your assistance in driving Danshaku Sandā off. He will return, in time. I hope to have a full holographic array in place before then." She turned her attention to Kara. "If you will allow me to keep your device, of course."

"Of course," Kara said. "But if you need any help, you know where to find us."

"I do," Doctor Sparx said. She handed Kara a small black notebook. "And you'll find me in here under Iteration 8102482. I've included a few other iterations I'm familiar with as well, and you can add your own in time."

Kara smiled. "It's been a pleasure working with you, Doctor Sparx."

"Likewise, Kara Sparx. Until we meet again." Doctor Sparx

pressed a few buttons on a handheld device and a portal shimmered to life a few meters in front of Kara, Lumien, and Snowflake.

Kara moved toward the portal, and her friends hurried to walk beside her. She looked sidelong at Snowflake before they reached the portal. "So, there's a 'nuthouse' me? Tell me more."

.

BLAST FROM THE PAST

Huntsman made the mistake of looking down while jumping from one rooftop to the other. It didn't keep him from making the jump, but it elicited laughter from Libertine, already on the roof he landed on. She and Kensei always made the leaps look easy, what with Libertine's telekinetic powers and Kensei's martial art and parkour training.

He sighed as he looked at them, but before he said anything, a flash of motion below caught his attention. He raised one gloved fist to signal the other two heroes to stop and then crouched at the edge of the roof. On the street below, an eight-foot-tall man dressed in nineteenth-century style clothing goose-stepped his way toward a storefront.

Libertine joined Huntsman at the edge of the roof. "What is that?"

"It looks like an oversized version of Chester Arthur," Huntsman replied.

Kensei joined the other two heroes. "How do you know this stuff?"

Huntsman shrugged. "I read a lot. And there's no mistaking those mutton-chop sideburns."

"Fair," Libertine said. "But you still haven't answered my question."

"If I had to guess, I'd say robot, between the way it moves, and the size."

"Then I'll ask the follow-up," Kensei said. "Why?"

"That remains to be seen," Huntsman said.

Libertine sighed. "We live in Cobalt City. I feel pretty safe saying that if there's a robotic version of an ex-president, it's probably not just for entertainment purposes."

As if to punctuate her point, the figure on the street held out its hands, palms forward, revealing wide-bore gun barrels in each. Large projectiles shot out. The ensuing explosion's heat reached the three heroes on the rooftop.

"Why must I always be right?" Libertine grumbled as she leapt from the rooftop.

Kensei hooked her grapple to the edge of the roof and shrugged at Huntsman. "She has a point," she said before rappelling down the side of the building.

Huntsman hooked his own grapple to the rooftop and descended. Libertine's mention of ex-presidents nagged at the back of his mind. He was certain there was something in the files the previous Huntsmen had collected over the centuries.

He reached the ground as some sort of force pulse from the figure's hands flung Libertine and Kensei backward.

"Robot," Libertine groaned as she rose.

Huntsman gave her a curt nod and nocked an arrow with an exploding tip. "Stand back."

The two women waited, poised to rejoin the battle, as Huntsman loosed his arrow. Though it struck the Chester Arthur robot in the chest, the explosion did not even mar the surface of its painted white shirt.

"Uh, thoughts?" Kensei asked.

"Looked like some sort of force field from this angle," Huntsman said.

Kensei's eyes narrowed. "I could try talking to the spirit, but it doesn't look too friendly."

Libertine nodded as she listened. "Okay, so let's find what's generating the force field, take that out. You wanna draw it?"

Kensei chuckled nervously. "Uh, sure." She crouched as she ran toward the robot, providing only a small target. As she neared its feet, she lashed out with her katana and then leapt away from the robot and her compatriots.

Libertine took advantage of the robot's momentary distraction to dash in the opposite direction Kensei was rolling. "Over here,

Walrus!"

The robot spun around at Libertine's voice, allowing Huntsman to check for a concealed power switch. "I don't see anything that looks like it's powering a force field." He fired another exploding arrow between the robot and Libertine.

The robot turned away from the explosion and marched in Kensei's direction again. Kensei ran toward the robot in a zig zag pattern. When she drew near, she jumped into the air and kicked at the robot's head. Her blow was ineffectual. A pulse from the robot threw her back fifty feet, and she slid across the pavement.

"K, are you alright?" Huntsman asked, firing an arrow between the robot and Kensei.

Kensei lifted one arm with her thumb up. "I think I'm just gonna sit this one out, guys," she croaked.

"I don't feel so great about this either," Libertine said, now beside Huntsman. "Is there anyone else available to help?"

"Stardust took his family to some amusement park down in the Carolinas. Gato Loco and Snowflake are on the West Coast. Archon ..." He trailed off. "Eh, it's worth a shot." He tapped his earpiece. "Call Gallows."

Libertine nudged Huntsman out of the way of an incoming blast. "Well, now we've got his attention. Talk fast, and tell Gallows to get Archon out here ASAP."

The line had connected just before Libertine barked her order, and Gallows sighed. "What have you gotten yourself into now, Huntsman?"

"Just a robot issue. Are you and Archon occupied?" He ducked a stray shot, but Libertine now drew most of the robot's fire, using her telekinesis to hover and dodge the blasts.

"He's out. I'm here, but I'm not sure what I can offer at the moment. We're fresh out of secure subterranean locations where I might lock up a robot."

"Alright, then any tips on stopping a robot with no obvious off switch?" Huntsman watched Kensei run across a nearby alley, pulling the robot's attention away from Libertine. Kensei faded into the shadows as soon as she reached the opposite side. The robot wheeled to again focus its attentions on Libertine.

"EMP?"

Huntsman sighed. "Must have left that in my other pants."

"Never leave home without one of those, man." Gallows

paused. "Ummm, what about something metal in its joints?"

"Something metal like arrows or a katana blade?"

"No, no, smaller than that. Like metal shavings."

"Okay, where would I get those on short notice?"

"Machinists' shop anywhere nearby?" Gallows suggested.

Huntsman grinned for the first time that night. "That I can work with. Thanks, man!"

"Don't mention it. And tell Libertine she'd better ask extra nice the next time she needs me to get her out of a jam."

Kensei rejoined Huntsman, popping out of the shadows just as seamlessly as she had vanished across the street.

"Will do." Huntsman disconnected the line. "Okay, we have a plan." He gestured down a block. "Kensei, can you make it down to the Harrington Auto Repair shop? We need some metal filings."

"Sure, how much?"

"Whatever you can find fast and bring back."

Kensei nodded and ran off. Libertine swung back around to where Huntsman stood. "What, Gallows is too busy for us?"

"No, Archon is unavailable, and Gallows doesn't know what he could contribute. By the way, he's none too pleased with you at the moment."

"So I'll send him another shipment of coffee," Libertine said, rolling her eyes. She shoved both hands forward, deflecting a blast from the robot into the corner of a nearby building. As the brickwork crumbled, she said, "He'll be fine. Geez, if I got mad every time someone needed me to use my powers, would you keep me around?"

"I'd keep you around even if you don't use your powers," Huntsman said with a shrug. "Speaking of, will your telepathy work on this thing?"

"No mind for me to cloud." She paused as she psychically tugged down a street sign and interposed it between the robot and the two heroes. "And yes, I checked."

"Good," Huntsman said.

Kensei's voice came over their communicators. "Got the shavings. What do I do with these?"

Libertine grinned at Huntsman. "Gallows comes through after all. Make it rain," she said. "You get them in the air, and I'll funnel them straight toward this Walrus."

~

The screech of metal on metal nearly drowned out Lumien's warning to Kara Sparx. She ducked just in time to avoid a fist swung in her direction. Judging by the inches-deep indentation it left in the bricks behind where her head had been, the bearer of said fist was probably more than human.

As Kara took to the skies, she cycled her goggles through various settings. "Lumien, are you seeing what I'm seeing?"

"Affirmative, Kara. The assailant is a robot." Lumien paused, an unusual humming on the open line. Kara suspected he was trying to emulate a "hmm," but his robotic voice hadn't been configured for such human speech intricacies. "It appears the technology is a rather antiquated design."

"Well, that's always good to hear." She dodged a flurry of energy pulses from the robot's eyes. "Hang on, why does that robot look like Nixon?"

"I do not know," Lumien replied.

"That's not much help, Lumien. Can you find anything on villains using robotic Nixons in Cobalt City?" Kara flew higher, out of the range of the blasts. "Particularly robotic Nixons who shoot lasers from their eyes?"

Lumien hummed again. Kara sighed. While an evolving AI had its benefits, Lumien had a tendency to pick up annoying habits. Including occasionally falling in love with her. She didn't want to have to wipe his memory banks again, but it looked inevitable. "I find no mention of robotic Nixons ..." He trailed off into static.

Kara glanced down. The robot Nixon had closed on Lumien's position, despite Lumien's electronic cloaking device. Though she couldn't identify what the attacker had done, Lumien's large glowing eye had gone dim.

She fired a blast from her zap gun, but it only caused a quick tracery of electricity to run across the robot's shoulder. If she got closer, it might have more of an impact, but then she opened herself up to more blasts. Still, she had no idea what this robot wanted with her or Lumien.

She flew in closer, adjusting the settings on her zap gun as she neared the robot Nixon. Just before she reached the edge of its range, she fired again. The sparks across the robot's carapace were more evident now, but Nixon did not slow. Kara fired the thrusters on her jetpack and flew up and away. At least now she had the thing's attention.

"Lumien, are you alright?"

Her robot's response was feeble. "I am not at full capacity."

"Head back to the van. I'm going to try an EMP, and I don't want you caught in the area."

"It may take me several minutes to reach the van."

"That's fine. Just let me know when you're there."

Kara dipped down within range of the robotic version of Nixon, evading its attacks while shooting at the robot's bulk. It was not quite as large as Lumien, but still towered to about seven or eight feet, far larger than the actual president had been.

After several minutes of drawing the robot farther from the van, the communication channel opened again. "Returned. Diverting power to shields."

Kara spun the dial on her zap gun and flew straight toward the robot on the ground. The robot did not fire at her, and she nearly aborted her attack run, in case it was planning a counter-attack. The moment the robot's eyes glowed red, she fired.

The beam from the zap gun stopped the robot in its tracks. She landed and approached it cautiously, but it didn't move. "We need to get this back to the lab. Are you good to drive?"

"Negative. Engaging automated driving."

Kara grinned. "That'll work."

~

Huntsman nudged the fallen robot with his toe. Though the shavings had not shut it down, they had frozen its joints enough that it was no longer a threat, at least for the moment.

On the left side of the robot's face, hidden beneath the muttonchop sideburn, he located the power button. As his gloved fingers brushed across it and stopped the robot's twitching, he frowned. He removed his glove and ran his fingertips over the button.

"Come feel this," he said.

Libertine took him up on the request, peering through the wiry fake hair on the side of the robot's face. "It looks like a starburst."

"Yeah, but not like a Star*Com thing. It looks more like ... a spark," Kensei said.

"Can you tell if its spirit has a connection to anyone in the city?" Huntsman asked.

Kensei shook her head. "It's rare that it works like that. I can look for places in the city that have a similar spirit attached to them, but that'll take me a while."

Huntsman shook his head. "No need, but if you happen across anything, let me know. You've still got to get to Regency Heights before tomorrow night, don't you?"

"Ugh, don't remind me," Kensei said. She slipped her cell phone out of a hidden pocket in her costume and glared at the face of it. "But I can knock that out tonight and be done with it."

"I'll come with you, just in case," Libertine said. She turned back to Huntsman. "I assume you've got cleanup covered?"

"Yeah, no problem," Huntsman said. "You girls have fun."

Libertine and Kensei both rolled their eyes before they walked away.

As soon as the two women were out of earshot, Huntsman pulled out his own cell phone and opened a connection with Stardust's database of Cobalt City heroes, seeking out the phone number of a sometimes hero who made the city her home.

~

"Hello?" Kara said. She didn't recognize the number the call came from, but Lumien, now restored to full power, assured her it was an old Protectorate phone number.

"Miss Sparx?" The voice on the other end was male, young, and not one Kara recognized.

"You've got her. Who am I speaking with?"

"Huntsman. I find myself in need of some robotics expertise."

Kara sighed. "What, is Stardust not available?"

"Well, he's not, actually. And, to be fair, he's more of a general technical person. You're a bit more specialized."

"Huh, flattery. I can accept that. Is this about a robotic Nixon?"

"No, robotic Chester A. Arthur."

Kara frowned. "Well that's odd."

"What made you think Nixon?"

"I've got a robotic Nixon in my lab right now. Uh, that is, I mean, I didn't build it. I was attacked, and I knocked it out, more or less."

No response came from Huntsman's end of the line for a moment. "Did you happen to find the power switch on yours?"

"No, I used an electromagnetic beam. It's like an EMP, only more directed."

"That would make things much easier, I suppose. Can you ... would it be alright if I brought the robotic Arthur to you? Any location in the city is fine."

"Assuming your robotic ex-president is the same size as my robotic ex-president, do you have something large enough to transport it?"

"Not on me. But I can arrange transportation." Huntsman paused. "Unless you've got a way?"

"I've got a van. Where should I pick you up?"

"Seventeenth and Grayson. And if you can keep it a little on the quiet side, the press isn't crawling all over this yet. It might be good if they aren't made aware of the altercation that just occurred."

"Suits me. I'll be there shortly."

~

Kara stared at the internal workings of the robotic replica of Chester A. Arthur. She wasn't sure how to react to Huntsman observing her. She hadn't worked with him before. In fact, it was a little odd he had called her, even with Stardust out of the city. She expected someone like Huntsman had a robotics expert on retainer, if the rumors about his family's wealth were to be believed.

She also wasn't sure how best to phrase the conclusion she had come to.

"So, it's a bit primitive, but there are a few things in here that are impressive. There are some parts that look a lot like--" She paused and chewed at her lip. "Well, some stuff I've built."

"Like?"

"Nothing that would attack a random storefront. The only robot I have is for technical assistance." She paused as her gaze slid toward the van, where Lumien waited. She shrugged. "Anyway, if it had been me, I'd have gone with Lincoln. Everybody likes Lincoln. Maybe Washington."

Huntsman nodded. "There's something else you should see." He pointed to the small spark-like indentation beneath the robot's sideburn. "Does that look familiar?"

"It looks like a spark, if that's what you're implying. But I don't sign my work. That's gauche."

Huntsman chuckled softly. "Is it possible this came from another iteration?"

Kara clenched her teeth and sucked in a deep breath. "Possibly made by an evil me?"

Huntsman's mouth opened and closed a few times before he spoke. "Are you aware of evil versions of yourself on another world?"

"I haven't met one, no. But I've made one foray into another iteration. With infinite worlds, the odds say one of them is home to evil Kara." She shrugged. "I'm old enough to remember when the evil Protectorate tried to destroy Cobalt City. I do worry that someday evil me might show up."

"I understand. Can you get the robot off the street, and see what you can find out if you disassemble it? I've got some research I need to do."

"Of course. Ah, you've got my number, and I guess I've got yours?"

"Yes." He paused. "I assume you know it's untraceable?"

Kara put her hands up. "Yeah. And I get that you're big on the secret identity thing. I won't pry." *Much.*

~

Kara's phone rang before she had even gotten the robot apart.

"Huntsman? I didn't expect to hear from you so soon."

"I found the information I was looking for. If I told you I have reason to believe that robot was constructed in 1976, or thereabouts, does that change your assessment?"

Kara whistled. "Yes, yes it does. In that case, color me impressed." She frowned. "Wait, that's a rather specific year. Bicentennial?"

"You got it. I'm sending you some photos of what I found. The inventor was a Doctor Funken."

Kara fumbled her phone, which fortunately muffled the stream of curse words interspersed with yelps that came from her. When she composed herself, she said, "Sorry, did you say Doctor Funken?"

"Yes. Does that name mean something to you?"

"How much German do you know?"

"Ein bisschen."

"*Sehr gut.* Funken means sparks. It's ... my great-grandfather's name was Funken in Germany. My grandfather changed it when he married my grandmother. Something about great-grandpa hiding out from the Russians."

"Really?" Huntsman asked. He sounded more surprised than incredulous, while Kara had always felt the latter about her great-grandfather's alleged adventures.

"I never knew if he was actually hiding out, or if it was just how a lot of Germans fled after the Nazis were defeated. I mean, I don't think he was a Nazi, but some good people did get forced into the service of the Nazis."

"I had a ..." Huntsman began, but trailed off. "One of the previous Huntsmen helped smuggle a German rocket scientist out from under the noses of the Russians. Did your family ever talk about how your great-grandfather got to America?"

"Not really, no. He died when I was young, so I got the second and third hand versions of the story."

Huntsman remained quiet after Kara finished. "I've found something. Sure enough, Doctor Funken. 1946. The Huntsman who operated in Europe during the war seems to have escorted him and his wife to Cobalt City."

"My grandpa was born in 1947, in Cobalt City." Now it was Kara's turn to go silent. "So, does that mean my great-grandfather was an evil mad scientist who made ex-president death-bots?"

"Yes to the made ex-president robots part. It looks like they were created for the Bicentennial celebration, and then warehoused ... it's a Quayside address. I'll call Libertine and Kensei, and we can go check it out."

Kara bit her lip. She didn't like volunteering for super hero outings, but if this had something to do with her great-grandfather, she had a moral obligation to help Huntsman sort it out. "I can go," she blurted. "You know, if they're busy."

"If you're available, I'd be happy to have you along. Especially if you can bring your EM ... well, the beam version of an EMP. Whatever you call it."

"I haven't thought of a good name for it yet. But yeah, I can bring it."

~

Kara nodded at Huntsman before she slid open the side door on the van. "Technical assistance," she said, inclining her head toward Lumien. "In a pinch, though, he's not horrible in a fight. I call him Lumien."

"Pleasure to meet you, Lumien," Huntsman said, approaching the van with his hand extended. "I'm ..."

"Huntsman. One of many to have borne that title," Lumien chirped. "I look forward to assisting you and Kara this evening."

"Right." Huntsman gave Lumien a stiff smile, then turned to regard the warehouse. "I checked the property records on the way over. It's owned by a holding company, and it looks like it's been rented out by the City ever since the Bicentennial. So it might just be that someone's stolen the robots from here."

Kara looked at Lumien. "Showtime, big guy."

Lumien climbed out of the van and rose to his full ten feet. His eye pulsed, and he said, "There are seven individuals within the building at present. Based on their locations, I believe four of them are security guards. The remaining three are in a room near the northwest corner of the building."

"Northwest," Huntsman murmured. "That's probably near the dock." He grinned at Kara and rubbed the back of his neck. "Okay, I know you invent things, but can you give me a quick summary of strengths and weaknesses? Yours and Lumien's?"

Kara looked at Huntsman. His posture reminded her of someone, but she couldn't place it. Everyone in Cobalt City knew the Huntsmen all came from one of the oldest and wealthiest families in town, but few agreed on which family. Kara had done light shows for a number of their parties. He could have been any of them.

"I fly with my jetpack and shoot things with my zap guns. One of which is currently reconfigured to shoot an electromagnetic beam that can take down a robotic ex-president at close range. Lumien is my eyes and ears. But he can take a hit a lot better than I can. Oh, and he's got the same sort of hologram projection that Snowflake has." She smiled. "Except Lumien's got the newest prototype."

Huntsman looked up. "Awesome. Can you get me to the roof?"

"I can't promise the most graceful landing, but yes. You've got an idea?"

"You and me up top, Lumien as our eyes and ears down here. Maybe disguised as a security guard?"

Lumien nodded and his appearance flickered into a non-descript man in a blue uniform and jacket.

"What do you have on mind for me on the roof?" Kara asked. "I'll be out of range for my beam up there."

"We stay out of sight until we're needed. I can shoot from up there, and you can fly down if need be."

"Great," Kara said, peering past Huntsman. "And what do we do if they spot us before we get out of sight?"

Huntsman spun and saw three robotic ex-presidents--Franklin Pierce, Andrew Johnson, and James Buchanan, from the looks of it--emerging from a roll-up door on the loading dock. "I guess I draw their fire and you get around behind them?"

Kara nodded and fired up her jetpack. As Huntsman scrambled to the left, she flew to the right and then up, heading for an elevation out of the robots' range. Before she got there, her legs tingled and then went numb. The last traces of electricity crackled across her legs when she looked down, and she saw a second bolt headed in her direction. She managed to evade the bulk of it, but her modified zap gun tumbled from her twitching hand as it was hit.

"That's dirty pool," she muttered. She tried to shake the numbness from her hand, but it persisted. "Gun down," she called. "I'm going higher to tweak the other one."

Huntsman nodded as he loosed an arrow at the Andrew Johnson robot. On impact, it released a net that entangled the robot's arms and legs. It wasn't enough to knock Johnson down, but it at least slowed it. Pierce and Buchanan approached Huntsman, and he hastily loosed two more arrows. The nets deployed off their marks, and barely slowed the robots.

As he scrambled backward, a mecha materialized between Huntsman and the robots. The robots opened fire on the mecha, and it lifted its arms to ward off the blasts. The laser beams went straight through the mecha, but it did not falter. Though Lumien as a security guard wasn't anywhere nearby, Huntsman suspected he had the robot to thank for the diversion. He took a moment to line up his shot, and then fired two more arrows, engulfing both Pierce and Buchanan in nets. Then he turned his attention skyward, scanning for Kara.

Kara flew upward as she adjusted the settings on her zap gun. The single gun and three targets made this dangerous, but a strafing run past the three robots was within her capabilities. Gun adjusted, she redirected her jetpacks and began a nosedive toward the robots on the ground. All three were fumbling with Huntsman's nets, which put the element of surprise on her side. She swept past them and zapped each one with her electromagnetic beam, grinning as they slowed.

Huntsman nodded to Kara as she landed. "That's pretty effective."

"Yeah," Kara said, scooping up her other gun from the ground. "But I think it's safe to say that forty-year-old robots don't just get up and attack without motivation." She nodded toward the warehouse. "My guess is that whoever is inside knows we're here now, so we'd better move fast."

"Kara, I have located the humans inside," Lumien chirped across the communicator.

"Show me," she said aloud. When Huntsman looked at her, she grinned. "Lumien's on the inside."

Huntsman frowned. "I thought he was out here directing the mecha."

"Mecha?" Kara laughed. "Yeah, he would use a mecha. But he can remote generate those from a device we have in the van."

"Oh, okay."

Kara turned her attention back to her AR display, which showed Lumien's view of the inside of the warehouse. "Three people, like we thought. I'm gonna go out on a limb and assume the one with crazy hair is the mad scientist who brought these robots out of mothballs." She breathed an internal sigh of relief that none of the people inside looked like any of her family members.

"Any indication of powers or devices?" Huntsman asked.

"Well, spotting powers only works if they're active. What do you think, Lumien?"

"There are a number of devices in the room aside from the robots, but none of the humans appear to be in possession of any devices. And you are correct about the possibility of powers."

Kara conveyed Lumien's report to Huntsman. "Do you have a

communications system I can link into?" she asked him.

Huntsman hesitated. "Yeah, that would be easier." He tapped his wrist, activating some device obscured by his sleeves. "It's active."

Kara set her communication network to locate Huntsman's, and nodded when he was on the network.

"How many more robots have you seen, Lumien?" Huntsman asked after Kara's nod.

"Thirty-two."

Kara breathed in sharply. "Seriously?"

"Makes sense," Huntsman said. "There had been thirty-eight presidents by 1976."

"You dealt with Arthur, I dealt with Nixon, and we took down these three. Plus thirty-two inside. How do you get thirty-eight?"

"Grover Cleveland. President twice, in non-consecutive terms. I assume they only made one Cleveland-bot."

"How do you know all of this?" Kara asked.

"I like trivia," he said. "Lumien, are all thirty-two active and patrolling?"

"No, there are currently no other active robots in the building."

Huntsman looked at Kara and shook his head. "Your robot is a bit literal." He returned to the communications channel. "So we can just walk in and head for the three humans?"

"Your path should be clear. Transmitting a map to Kara's AR now."

"Wow, you have AR?"

Kara grinned. "Top of the line. My own design, of course. I've got the path. Ready to roll?"

"Lead on," Huntsman said.

Kara walked through the open loading dock entry. As soon as she had crossed the threshold, the door began to roll down, threatening to separate Huntsman from her. He charged toward the entry, squeezing in as the door reached a point lower than the top of his head.

"What the heck?" he muttered.

As the door closed, a blinding light shone at both of the heroes. A crackle preceded an amplified feminine voice. "Welcome, Miss Sparx. So kind of you to join us."

Kara looked at Huntsman, eyes wide. "Did I just fall for a supervillain trap?"

He shrugged in response, his bow already in one hand and his other hand hovering near his quiver.

Kara drew both of her zap guns. "Who have I joined?" she called.

"Call us the New Revolution. We plan to be a positive force for change in Cobalt City, and we seek your assistance."

"Positive force for change by attacking with robotic ex-presidents? How does that make sense?"

"It got you to notice us, did it not?"

Huntsman stepped near to Kara and muttered, "Keep her attention. I've got an idea." He moved toward the side of the door without waiting for Kara's response, and fiddled with the control panel.

Kara watched him for a moment, but then returned her attention to the disembodied voice. "Okay, so why did you want me to notice you?" She sighed. "And if your answer is that you were jilted in college or something, I assure you, you've got the wrong woman."

"Your family name was not always Sparx, was it?"

"Damn," Kara muttered under her breath. She looked over at Huntsman. His response was a thumb's up, but without seeing his eyes, she couldn't tell if that meant he was making progress or she should keep going. "No, it was Funken before."

"And Doctor Berthold Funken was the mastermind behind these brilliant robots. We want you to help us unlock their full potential."

"Wait, you want me to believe my great-grandfather made bicentennial death-bots?"

"No, he provided us the shells for our agents of change. But his specialty was not in the field of robotics. It was rocketry, propulsion. He must have used some of that knowledge in the creation of these robots."

Kara chuckled. "Look, I never met the man, but I can tell you this much. Once he got to America, he took jobs that paid. No one in Cobalt City wanted rockets. They wanted things that were functional or decorative. So that's what he made. I don't think these robots hide any big secrets."

Kara trailed off as the light winked out. Eight pairs of glowing red dots, roughly seven feet off the ground, illuminated the now darkened loading bay. "Uh, Huntsman?"

"I got ..." he said. "Oh. Well, the good news is this New Revolution can't get out of the building until I unlock the entries. The bad news is we can't get out of here until I, well, do that same unlocking thing."

"Right." Kara leveled both of her zap guns. "Listen, New Revolu ... um, tionaries, or whatever you want to be called. You've seen what I can do with my guns, correct? I will shoot down all thirty-two of your remaining ex-presidents if I have to. Or you can tell them to stand down, and not attack two of Cobalt City's heroes. Again."

The loudspeakers overhead crackled again, then fell silent.

"I'm gonna take that as a no," Kara said as she fired at the line of glowing eyes. The shielding around the robots shimmered in the glow of her electromagnetic beams a moment before they hit. "Down!"

Huntsman ducked as Kara fell prone. The beams bounced off the shield and flew over the heads of the two heroes. They impacted the rolling door instead of their targets.

Kara fiddled with her goggles, but they did not flicker to life. "Lumien?"

Her robot's voice came back distorted, as though over a great distance. "Where are you, Kara?"

"My visuals are down. Do you have anything?"

"Negative. There was a flash just before they ceased functioning. I believe it is some sort of cloaking mechanism."

"Ugh, why do they get the cool toys?" she grumbled. She turned to Huntsman. "Thoughts?"

"If we could see what's generating their shields, we could target that."

"Unless they're what's generating it. Hmm, thought. Fire an arrow, but low, just in case it ricochets."

An arrow whooshed across the darkened space and clattered against the floor before it tinked off something metallic. Huntsman chuckled. "Force field, not ballistic armor."

Kara nodded as she fired up her jet pack. "P.S., if Snowflake ever asks, I did *not* fly indoors. Personal point of pride with that damn panda." She lifted off and arced to the side of the line of robots, then pushed the thrusters to their maximum and barreled into the side of the robot on the end of the row. As soon as her shoulder impacted metal, she fired her zap guns indiscriminately.

Five of the eight robots fell in her first pass.

"Seven-ten split," Huntsman said with a chuckle. "You want me to shoot cleanup?"

"If by cleanup, you mean nets, then be my guest." Kara hovered near the ceiling of the warehouse and awaited the sound of three shots. Then she flew back down and plugged each of the robots with a single shot.

"CCPD is on their way," Huntsman said as Kara landed. "You know, we make a pretty good team."

"Thanks," she replied, "but I'm not so cut out for this heroic stuff."

ABOUT THE AUTHOR

Dawn Vogel has been published as a short fiction author and an editor of both fiction and non-fiction. By day, she edits reports for and manages an office of historians and archaeologists. In her alleged spare time, she runs a craft business and tries to find time for writing. She lives in Seattle with her awesome husband (and fellow author), Jeremy Zimmerman, and their herd of cats. For more of Dawn's work, visit http://historythatneverwas.com/.

ABOUT THE ILLUSTRATOR

Luke Spooner a.k.a. 'Carrion House' currently lives and works in the South of England. Having recently graduated from the University of Portsmouth with a first class degree he is now a full time illustrator for just about any project that piques his interest. Despite regular forays into children's books and fairy tales his true love lies in anything macabre, melancholy or dark in nature and essence. He believes that the job of putting someone else's words into a visual form, to accompany and support their text, is a massive responsibility as well as being something he truly treasures. You can visit his web site at www.carrionhouse.com.